Cover Art by Stephanie at Bus Stop Shop

Editing by R.N. Barbosa at Barbos Books

Proofreading by Annmarie at Chapter by Chapter Editing

Trigger Warnings

This is a dark romance. Some content may be disturbing and/or triggering to some readers.

This book includes: stalking, murder, domestic violence, torture, blood, and discussions of mafia activity. There are also instances and discussions of men being shitty and abusive.

There are sexually explicit scenes in this book, including kinks such as Daddy kink, mask kink, impact play, pet play, anal, scissoring, choking/gagging, edging/orgasm denial, bondage, praise and degradation, knife play, getting turned on during a Pap smear, foot play, primal play, and use of sex toys. There are also instances of dubious consent and consensual non-consent.

A Note from the Author

Hi there. Thank you so much for picking up my dark sapphic romance. I wanted to take a minute to address something that may come up as you read the book. As you learn about Blair and Danielle, you may find yourself thinking, "This character has the characteristics of [insert mental health issue here]." I want to be clear that I am not providing a diagnosis for either character or for their behaviors. This book is not meant to be an accurate depiction of any mental health concern.

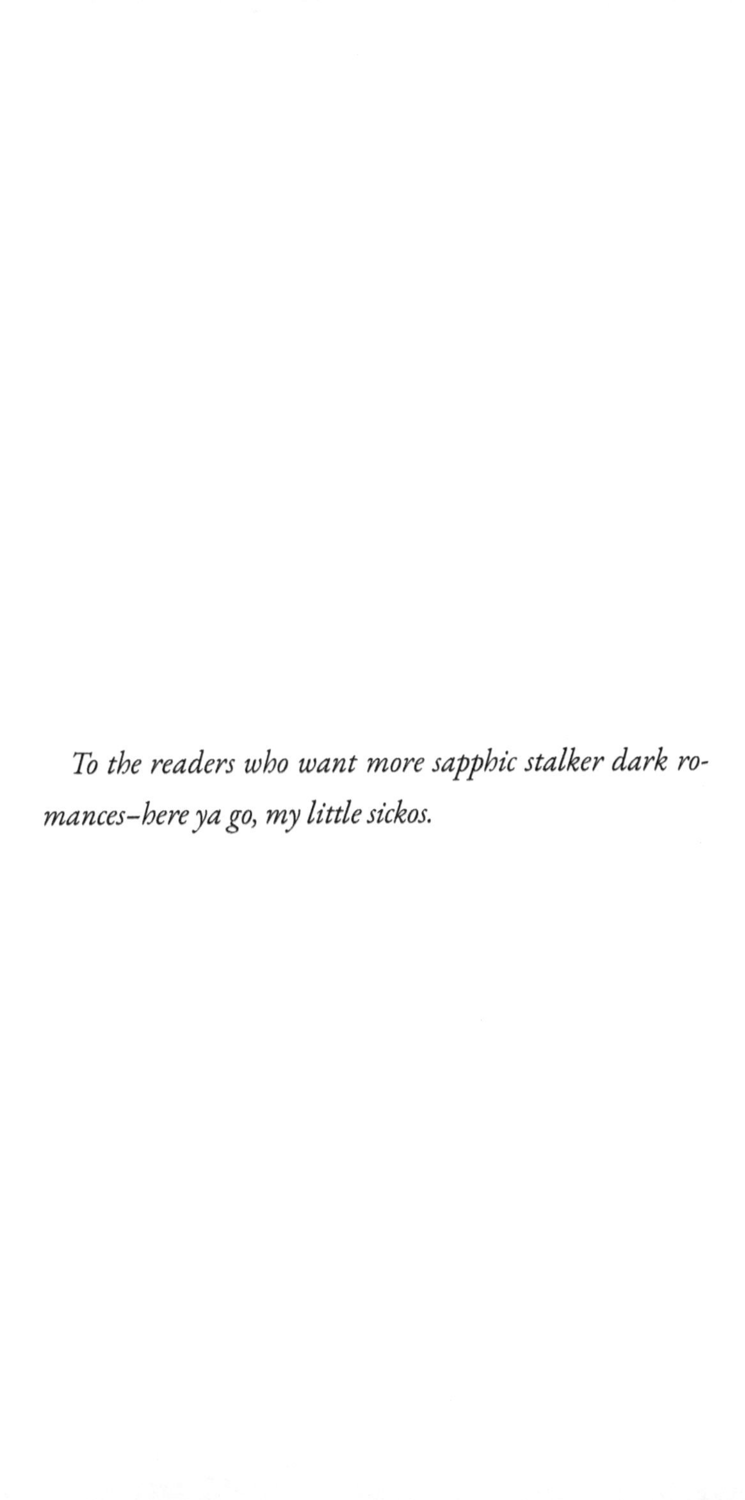

To the readers who want more sapphic stalker dark romances—here ya go, my little sickos.

Prologue

"Come on, baby, let's get more comfortable."

I nearly roll my eyes at this man giving me a pet name so quickly, but I force a smile instead. We matched on Tinder a few days ago and skipped the small talk, going straight to meeting up.

There's only one goal for tonight.

We're sitting on his stained couch, the cushions sunken from overuse. I don't even want to know what treasures are hidden underneath them. His place is a mess: empty liquor bottles on the dirty coffee table in front of us, clothes thrown over nearly every surface...and don't even get me started on his baseboards.

He positions himself so that he's laying down, his back pressed against the frame with his head at one end and his feet at the other. I follow suit, becoming the little spoon as the TV continues playing *The Godfather* before us. I've never actually watched this movie, and don't plan to now, but he put it on without bothering to ask for my input.

It doesn't really matter. Neither of us are really watching it.

He moves his arm so I can lay my head down, just as his other hand snakes around my breast. He kneads it roughly, triggering my irritation. Why must men be so aggressive about it?

"Like that, baby?" he asks, gyrating his hips against my backside.

"Mmhmm." I hope that sounded sexy instead of annoyed. I don't think he'd notice, anyway.

He groans in my ear as his hand finally leaves my chest alone and moves further south. "You wanna suck me off?"

I nearly make a *eugh* sound, because no, no I do not.

Do it now, the voice in the back of my head demands. *Do it now. Don't chicken out.*

Nerves wriggle in my stomach. Now that I'm here, with this man acting like a horny teenager, I'm scared. What if I fuck it up?

DO IT, the voice shouts.

Before I lose my nerve, I say, "Yeah," in a breathy tone. I flip myself over to face him. "Sit up."

His dark eyes are glazed over at the mere thought of getting his dick wet. He scrambles into a seated position, nearly throwing me from the couch in the process. I shuffle around to straddle him.

Do it, the voice croons. *This one will be good practice.* His brows furrow as I settle over him.

"Uh—"

He doesn't have time to demand I get to my knees before my forehead smashes into his nose. A sickening crunch fills my ears as his nose breaks. He howls in pain, bucking me off as he grips his nose.

"What the fuck?" he screams, blood gushing through his fingers.

He needs to shut the fuck up. I can't have anyone hearing him.

I take the vodka bottle from the coffee table and smash it over his head.

The bottle shatters as his head rears to the side, blood trickling down his temple. All he can manage is a pained groan as his eyes close and a hand reaches for his temple.

Panic starts to creep up my spine. Or is it excitement? I can't tell, but I don't have time to decide. I drop the handle of the destroyed bottle and pick up a new one, bringing it down upon him again until he's rendered unconscious.

I let out a sigh of relief. "This man is bad," I murmur to myself, to this seedy apartment, to the universe and any cosmic beings who might be listening.

He hurts women. He sent his ex-girlfriend to the hospital. She nearly died. When she got free, he showed up to her house and threatened her. He's dangerous and deserves to die.

The knowledge of who and what he is helps relax my muscles and cools my blood.

Then I begin.

Chapter 1
Blair

The Halloween festivities are in full swing.

My sister's home is decked out for the holiday. Spiderwebs cover the bushes, jack-o-lanterns are perched on the front steps, and a zombie doll that jumps at anyone who steps too close is set up on the lawn.

I'm not even at the stairs when the front door swings open and my seven-year-old niece rushes to me. "Auntie Blair!" She's dressed as a princess, a bright pink, tulle dress nearly swallowing her tiny frame. The tiara on her head is askew, barely holding onto her blonde hair as she makes her way over to me, throwing her arms around my waist. "It's Halloween!"

"It is," I reply, looking down at her. "You're dressed as a princess."

"I'm Princess Peach," she informs me proudly.

I'm about to tell her I'm unfamiliar with the royal family when I hear my sister open her screen door. I lift my eyes to see her very pregnant frame step onto the front porch, her second born, Jack, propped against her hip.

"Thanks for taking Emma," Ariana says, her voice strained. "I can barely make it down the street without needing to lie down. Not that lying down is very comfortable, either."

And your lowlife husband was too busy playing video games, I want to sneer, but hold my tongue. If this were just a few years ago, I would've said it, but I don't want her crying tonight.

Ariana is my half-sister—we have the same mother—but she isn't like me. She cries at the drop of a hat and has always been dramatic. It makes me wonder if my biological father is the reason for my lack of empathy.

My sister is a great person to study for human emotions, though, considering she never shies away from expressing them. I learned how to mimic emotional responses from her—although, I don't dial it up as much as she does. I want to be believable, after all.

I value having her and her children in my life despite not feeling things the way they do. I love my niece and nephew—at least, I think I do. I know I'd do anything for them, regardless of the consequences. I know I like having them in my life, but I don't feel anything—I don't get butterflies or feel warm when I look at them.

I can't think of a time where I've felt much of any-thing— anything besides anger, at least. I've felt anger plenty. But things like joy, sadness, longing? Those are foreign to me, even when I slip on my mask.

My family acts as my anchor, holding me back from shirking all expectations. I've disappeared from my life before, packing up and fucking off without a word simply because I could, but it had hurt my sister too much. When I finally showed up on her doorstep six months later, she threw a pan at my head and broke down in tears, babbling about how she thought I was dead.

I didn't want to deal with that again, so I've stayed put since.

Emma still clings to me, thrumming with excitement. I work to alter my face, to provide the mask of Normal Human, as I look down and ask, "Are you ready for some tricks?"

My niece shakes her head. "It's called trick-or-treating, Auntie Blair."

"That's what I said."

She gives me a giggle. "We have to go now! I want to find all the houses with the best candy."

As Emma starts listing her favorite treats, Ariana tells me, "Please bring her coat with you. She says it ruins her costume, but I don't want her getting sick," before disappearing into the house for a few moments.

Emma is still running through her list when my sister reappears with a hot pink children's coat in her other hand. Gently, I detangle from my niece and step towards my sister. "Don't worry, we won't get into *too* much trouble."

My sister snorts. "Just don't be out late, okay?"

"Yes, madam."

I take the coat from her and head back to grab Emma's hand, which she gladly takes, still talking my ear off as we make our way into the night.

The sidewalks are full of children, all various ages and dressed as various characters. Their shrieks and laughter fill the air around us, guiding us from one house to the next. Emma has no qualms marching up to each front door, so I hang back on the sidewalk.

I shove my hands into my coat pockets as I watch my niece like a hawk. The weather has taken a nosedive, throwing us into autumn with brute force. It's always jarring, going from seventy-degree days to fifty degrees nearly overnight.

Emma bounds over to me, showing me the contents of her pillowcase. "They were giving out full Snickers!"

"Ah," I reply. "Is that good?"

She gawks at me. "Auntie Blair, you really need to get out more." She thrusts her pillowcase towards me, seemingly demanding I hold it, and heads to the next house. Trailing after her, I observe it.

This house had a for sale sign out front until a month ago. Its ranch style is nearly identical to the rest of the homes in this neighborhood. The difference between this home and others, though, is the lack of Halloween decor. Only a few jack-o-lanterns sit on each porch step; no spiderwebs, no skeletons, no spooky lighting.

Perhaps that's why most of the children we pass seem to skip on this house. They probably assume there's no point.

Emma doesn't seem to mind, though, as she marches up the walkway and onto the porch. Something I can't quite name has me following closely behind her, my feet guiding me until I'm right in front of the door. My niece wastes no time banging her little fist against the door, shouting, "Trick or treat!" before there's even any sign that someone is home.

A few moments later, a woman swings open the door with the brightest smile I've ever seen. "Oh, my first trick-or-treater! Here, I have a whole bowl for you to choose from," she chirps before disappearing for a moment to retrieve the candy. Her smile hasn't left her face as she holds out the bowl. "Go ahead, take as many as you want."

"Woah," Emma breathes, ripping the bowl from the woman's hands and sitting on the porch.

As Emma inspects the candy, I inspect the woman across from me. "You're new to town," I state.

The woman nods, her dark curls bouncing with the movement. "I just moved here about a month ago. It's been quite a whirlwind."

"If you wanted more trick-or-treaters, you should have decorated more," I advise, finding myself drawn into the depthless pools of her dark eyes.

She blinks, her smile dropping slightly. "Oh, sorry. Yeah, I know it's a pathetic display. I have a bunch of decorations somewhere packed away, but I can't find them."

I tilt my head. "You don't label your boxes?"

Her cheeks turn a hint of pink. "No, I do—of course I do. I just, well, I couldn't find them." She gives a nervous laugh. "I'll be ready for Christmas, though, don't worry." She thrusts her hand out. "I'm Danielle, by the way."

This one is strange. I can't quite put my finger on it, but something is different about her. I scrutinize her, my eyes roving over her face.

Her eyes are so dark, they almost seem black, matching her dark hair. Her eyes sit under thick eyebrows and are accentuated by long eyelashes. Her nose is slightly crooked, leaning to the left side of her face—possibly from breaking it— and her bottom lip is a bit too big for the top. When she smiles, a dimple appears on her right cheek, but not her left.

She's not conventionally attractive, but there's something about her I find intriguing. Something that lurks under the surface, shoved into a box because it isn't allowed out.

She clears her throat, making me realize I've just been staring at her for what people might consider too long. "And what's your name?" she prompts, her hand still outstretched.

"My name's Emma," my niece says from the ground, still rummaging through the candy bowl.

Danielle gives her a stilted smile as she wipes her hand on her knit sweater, trying to play off what she considers an awkward moment. It's matched with a plaid skirt and fishnets hugging her legs.

Suddenly, her eyes shift as they lock back on me—a look mixed with annoyance and calculation. A look of someone who is sizing up a predator, not for fear of being prey, but to scrutinize an opponent.

Some primal instinct is trying to warn her, to tell her who stands before her.

"Can I take two Skittles?" my niece asks, oblivious to what is happening between this woman and me.

As quickly as it appeared, the look is gone as she blinks and takes in my niece. "You can take as many as you'd like. That is, if it's all right with your mom."

"I'm not her mother," I say at the same time Emma exclaims, "That's my Auntie Blair!"

"Oh," Danielle replies, her dark eyes locking with mine again. "Sorry—then yes, if it's okay with your Aunt Blair."

Emma doesn't bother responding, as she knows I don't care.

"Where did you move from?" I ask, searching her, trying to see beneath her mask some more.

"I moved from Ohio," she says a bit evasively. "I've always wanted to live here, though. I've always loved the weather, loved the mountains—although, I'm too afraid to live *in* the mountains. It would be just my luck that I buy a house that slides right off the side of one," she chuckles.

I hum noncommittally. She's a bit too chatty. Maybe she's nervous, which is a foreign feeling to those like me. Maybe I'm wrong about her.

Nonsense, the voice in my head whispers. *This is all a ruse.*

She has something hidden beneath the surface.

I've always excelled at finding others like me, but this one is tricky. It's as if the mask we're forced to wear is stuck to her face, as if she truly believes the mask is *her*.

She continues, "Also, I feel like the winters here compared to the ones at home are different, like the type of cold you get. Does that make sense? Have you experienced a Midwestern winter before?"

"No."

"Oh," she mumbles, her hands coming together to fiddle with her fingers. "Sorry, I get a bit talkative when I'm nervous."

"Why are you nervous?" I push, needing to figure this new puzzle out. Her choosing anxiousness to present to me is strange—we've never bothered with pretending to have that feeling.

"Just," she waves her hands around, "all of this. Moving, meeting neighbors, the whole thing."

"And you live here on your own?"

"Yep," she straightens a bit, as if proud of this fact.

I'm about to probe some more when Emma says, "All done! I took nine." She stands, turns, and marches down the steps, the bowl discarded behind her.

Danielle gives a small laugh. "Well, you and Princess Peach have a great rest of your Halloween. It was nice meeting you, Blair."

No, I nearly growl. I'm not done trying to understand this woman, to know what I'd find underneath the layers covering her true self. I want to drag my niece back up here just so I can keep digging.

She's already an enigma, just different enough from any other person who is just like me.

I take her in, letting myself get my fill before I nod and turn on my heel.

I'll be back, I tell myself. I have to know—I have to uncover who Danielle really is.

Chapter 2
Danielle

Halloween in my new home was exciting, even if I only got a handful of trick-or-treaters.

It's past midnight now, the families long gone, but I can't seem to settle. I sit in my living room, bundled under a pile of blankets, the TV playing some sitcom in the background as I nurse a glass of wine.

That strange woman unnerved me tonight. I'm not sure why, but a little voice in my head kept shouting, *danger! danger! danger!*

I've ignored that voice before, and I don't plan on repeating that mistake.

Still, for some reason, I felt the urge to overshare with her, which is silly. I need to be careful who I share things with—I can't trust anyone. Especially dangerous women.

I can't pinpoint what gives me pause about her besides her energy. She made me nervous, which isn't unusual for me. She probably thought I was some babbling idiot. The way her gray eyes burrowed into my skin, trying to figure me out, trying to throw me off-kilter. The way she acted aloof, but she had something just beneath the surface. A curiosity. A longing, maybe. But for what?

I need to pull myself together and stop fixating on things I've made up. Sighing, I drain my glass and get up, needing to go to bed at a reasonable hour instead of sitting around for far too long. I leave my little nest as it is, heading upstairs to my bedroom.

The necessities, like my bed and a few other pieces of furniture, are set up, but everything else is packed away in my basement. I've tried unpacking a few boxes every day, but I just end up overwhelmed and frustrated that I even need to unpack in the first place. Leaving my life behind was not what I had planned.

I head into my bedroom, skirting around my bed to reach the connected bathroom. Quickly going through my nighttime routine, I vow to unpack more shit this week. I know I didn't plan to leave everything, but that's what had to happen, so I need to just suck it up and unpack my kitchenware.

It's unfair, the voice in my head whispers. *It's unfair that he gets to live his life while I uproot mine.*

Resentment heats my blood.

I sigh through my nose as I begin to brush my teeth.

I wonder if this feeling will ever go away.

I drag myself out of bed and down to the kitchen, rubbing my bleary eyes as I head over to feed my betta fish. Swim Shady darts happily to his food pebbles, sucking them down before drifting into his little castle hideaway. Letting out a yawn, I mindlessly start my coffee machine.

I'll admit, it feels nice to be in my own home and not have to worry about anyone else.

I haven't been alone in a long time; if Jeremy wasn't physically around, he was constantly calling or texting, demanding to know what I was doing, where I was, and who I was with. Once he alienated me from my friends and family, I didn't feel alone then either, simply because he was always breathing down my neck. After I broke free of him, my abandoned friends took me in, but I hated living with other people.

For the first time in a long time, I'm on my own.

As the machine spits out my coffee, I pad over to the fridge for my oat milk coffee creamer and notice my fridge is basically empty, aside from the coffee creamer, the half-full bottle of wine, and a gluten free breakfast sandwich I got at a Celiac-friendly bakery in town. Sighing, I shut the door and move back to my cup on the counter.

"I'm heading to my first day today," I tell Swim Shady. "Would you like me to stop at a pet store on the way home? Maybe for some new accessories?"

His little head pops out, as if registering my question, before he glides to the top of his tank, searching for a treat.

"No, I'm not giving you more food," I scold, pouring my creamer. "No extra meals for you."

He dips back into his palace.

Slurping down my coffee, I place my mug in the sink and head upstairs to get dressed.

I take a few deep breaths as I ride the elevator to the twelfth floor, but it does nothing to soothe the nerves. After countless job applications, dozens of rejection emails, and ten different interviews, I finally secured a job offer. It's for a big-name marketing agency, although I've never worked in marketing before. Luckily, they weren't looking for that; the agency needed someone familiar with medical and public health research, and I fit that bill perfectly.

I'd much rather be working for an actual public health organization, but I can't afford to be picky. The job market blows. I applied to so many jobs, I don't even remember applying to this one. But they were eager to interview me, and I was eager to have money, so it worked out.

The elevator doors open before I can fully collect myself, but I step out into the hallway like I know what I'm doing, fighting the urge to fiddle with my cardigan. *Always walk with purpose,* my mother used to say. *It makes people think you're confident.*

I'm greeted by the woman who conducted my interview— Sarah? Kara? Fuck, I can't remember. She gives me a smile as she approaches, even as her eyes scrutinize my ensemble, which is a black dress and black tights, pulled together by studded Doc Martens. "Dani! So happy to see you. Welcome to the agency."

"Danielle," I correct automatically.

I never liked going by Dani, even as a child. Not that there's anything wrong with it; what's wrong is people assuming I should go by a nickname just because my actual name can be shortened.

She blinks in surprise, her smile faltering a bit as she replies, "So sorry, Danielle. Let me show you around."

I give her a wide smile, overcompensating for my social faux pas, even though I don't *really* think it is one. Trailing behind this woman, I mentally kick myself. I have no issues picking up on social cues, but sometimes I say the wrong thing or react in a way that others wouldn't. To fit in with others, I started noticing how others respond to things and try to mimic.

But sometimes it falls flat.

"We're so happy to have you join us," she tells me as we rush into the office.

It's almost a complete open concept layout, with long tables, a few cubicles in the center, and conference rooms with floor-to-ceiling windows bordering the space. There's no sense of privacy here.

"We used to just contract your position outside, but once we got the federal contract, they gave us funding to hire someone. It's perfect—the government can be real sticklers about what we say in our health marketing." I keep quiet, already bored. She keeps going, "As you can see, the office is completely open. It really helps build community and collaboration." I nearly snort, but rein it in. "If you need a conference room, you can request one through the online portal. IT will get your laptop set up."

"I won't have an assigned desk?" I ask.

"Oh no," she says emphatically. "We believe placing restrictions on our team, such as putting walls between us, halts creativity. You're welcome to sit anywhere that has an open seat!"

Oh my God, that's horrifying. I keep a smile plastered on my face while I berate myself for not asking about the office during the Zoom interview.

This is a disaster, the voice in my head growls.

Eyeing the people as they flit about the office, I notice that I stick out like a sore thumb. I tug on the hem of my black, knee-length dress self-consciously. I'm not a full-on goth, but I've always preferred a grungier look. That, mixed with my Resting Bitch Face, keeps most people at a distance. It gives off the vibe that I don't want to deal with them.

Because I don't.

The woman takes me back to the elevators. "Now, Human Resources and our fearless leaders have offices upstairs. No one really goes up there unless they have an appointment. I'll take you up to HR now, so you can finish up your paperwork." As we gather into the elevator and head up, she keeps rambling on about how this company thrives off late night meetings, constant brainstorming sessions, and the coffee bar down in the lobby.

I hate the sound of everything—minus the coffee. I didn't struggle to make friends when I was younger, and I know how to be sociable, but I'd just prefer to be alone. I didn't realize how much I enjoy solitude until I moved here, away from everyone and everything I knew. Now that I have it, I don't really want to let it go.

It'll be fine, I tell myself, trying to soothe the agitation already building in me. *Your job is different from what everyone else here does. They'll leave you alone.*

She's still blabbing on when we get off the elevator and round the corner. I'm so stuck in my own head that I don't see the person coming towards us until I've completely collided with them.

It feels like I've been zapped--energy flows through me as we make contact. My hands go out instinctively to shield myself, and my palms press into the person's very generous chest.

"Oh God," I exclaim and back up, my hands still outstretched. "I'm so—"

My eyes finally register who I've run into. Dark hair and gray eyes.

The woman from Halloween. Blair.

She looks even more intimidating today: her dark hair is glossy and straight, landing at her shoulders; her black dress shirt is tucked into her black trousers, covered by an open petticoat. Black, shiny heels make her a few inches taller, so now she's towering over me.

Heat immediately creeps up my neck as the woman guiding me squawks, "Ms. Erickson, we are so sorry about that! Are you okay?" She rushes towards Blair, as if she might touch her, but thinks better of it. "We didn't see you—but we should have! *I* should have—"

"It's quite all right," Blair interrupts, her stormy eyes ensnaring mine, making it feel like we're the only two people here. Her eyes dance with amusement. "I take it you're the new research specialist."

"I am," I breathe, trying to regain my composure. "Sorry about running into you."

Her mouth lifts at the corner. "No apology necessary. Just watch where you're going next time," she jokes before tilting her head. "I look forward to seeing your work."

I nod, still trapped in her eyes, until she steps around me, releasing me from her spell. She prowls down the hallway before reaching a door and stepping in, disappearing from view.

The woman's voice is like buzzing in my ear. I shake my head and look over at her. "Who is that?"

"That's Blair Erickson, one of our partners. She has a lot of sway and power around here, but isn't here regularly," she says shakily. "Which is good."

I furrow my brows. "Why is that good?"

"She's just...hard to read. She's very smart, and can really turn on the charm, but I never know what she's thinking. I hope we didn't upset her just now."

Huh. That's strange. Blair was clearly amused and joking around. I try to shrug it off as I'm led to HR—maybe this woman isn't very observant.

Chapter 3
Blair

My laptop pings with new email notifications, but I ignore them as I smile to myself. What a beautiful coincidence this has turned out to be.

It takes me barely any time to pull up her personnel file.

Danielle Taylor, thirty years old, from a small town in Ohio. According to her resume, she attended University of Illinois for the joint degrees of Bachelor of Science in Community Health and a Master of Public Health.

I lick my lips as I look over her forms. She's obviously brilliant, but if she's being truthful about her work experience, she doesn't stick it out for long—many of her previous jobs lasted less than a year.

First Halloween, now this? It's as if the universe is trying to force us together.

This is to help her, the voice in my head croons. *To help her see who she truly is.*

I'm curious how she will handle this atmosphere. It's fast-paced and demanding, with clients thinking they do the most important work in the world. Add that to the lack of privacy in this office, and you have a recipe for neuroticism.

She'll either wilt under the pressure, or she'll bloom. I expect the latter, if I'm right about her.

Her social media presence is lacking, which is fine. I don't need some sanitized version of her that everyone else sees. No, I want the raw, unfiltered version that I know is desperate to come out.

I sit back in my chair, a plan already forming in my mind. I know exactly what I need to do.

Chapter 4
Danielle

My day passes smoothly, but I'm drained by the end. It consisted of enduring many awkward introductions, sitting quietly in meetings I won't keep straight for a while, and having to pretend to be interested in small talk.

It was especially difficult because my mind kept wandering up one floor to that alluring woman. What a strange coincidence—we met on Halloween, and it turns out that she's my boss's boss's boss's...boss? I still don't really understand the chain of command.

And what what's-her-face said earlier, about not being able to read Blair, has nagged at me. From our very limited interactions, it's clear that Blair doesn't overly emote like people might be accustomed to, but her thoughts are written on her face. Someone would just have to know where to look.

I force myself to push it from my mind as I drive out of the building's parking lot, chalking it up to my coworker just not noticing.

My mind wanders to how nice it feels to be alone in my car. I have a feeling being stuck in this office will suck.

Not to toot my own horn, but I'm intelligent and I'm educated. I'm qualified for the jobs I apply for; my problem is staying.

I broke off the engagement to Jeremy two years ago, finally ready to break free of his abuse. It took him a while, but he eventually left me alone–no more showing up at my jobs, no more obsessively calling me in the middle of the night.

Until a few months ago.

For some reason, when he started up again, it was in full force. He began showing up unannounced at my work, freaking everyone out, which would lead to me getting let go—for the safety of my coworkers.

I understood the logic, but the anger and resentment kept growing with each job I lost.

But now I'm in a new state and he has no idea where I am, I remind myself as I pull into the grocery store's parking lot. He'll never show up here, even if he keeps finding my phone number and leaving me threatening voicemails. I'm safe from him.

I climb out of the car, the fall weather biting at my ankles as I rush inside. I haven't been to this store yet, but the Gluten Free Finder app I use said they have a lot of safe food options for me.

I wander down the aisles with my shopping cart, trying to find where the treasure might be kept. The store is packed, and I fight the urge to give people a dirty look when they leave their cart in the middle of the aisle.

I turn down the last aisle and nearly let out a gasp.

This store has a plethora of gluten free alternatives waiting for me.

Granted, most stores have jumped on the bandwagon, but this one has alternatives I haven't seen before. I can't stop myself from basically stroking a box of gluten free farfalle in awe.

Yeah, these are coming home with me.

I was diagnosed with Celiac Disease ten years ago, after struggling with stomach issues for as long as I can remember. It manifested into strange eating habits. I used to tear my peanut butter and jelly sandwiches into pieces, then eat them one by one. It wasn't until I was in college where my symptoms revved up—I'd eat a meal in the dining hall and get sick almost an hour later. My stomach always felt like it was going to explode. One night, I was dry heaving so heavily, I couldn't breathe and seriously considered calling 911.

Once I saw a doctor, one thing led to another, and I was slapped with the diagnosis. No more gluten for me. It didn't just alter my diet, though—it altered my life. I became increasingly paranoid about eating food prepared by anyone else. The only place I could trust to not encounter cross-contamination was my own kitchen. I became too anxious to go to restaurants or participate in any events that revolved around food.

It didn't help that Jeremy was constantly belittling me for my worries.

Fuck him, the voice in my head snarls as I place the box of pasta in my shopping cart. I hope he chokes on his 'regular' bread.

I'm too busy with my own thoughts to notice someone stepping up next to me.

"Sorry," I mumble, shuffling back before turning to look at them.

Gray eyes meet mine.

"Oh, hi there," I murmur to Blair, suddenly flustered under her intense gaze.

She tilts her head, as if studying me. Again. "Danielle," she says by way of greeting.

"Um, hi." I struggle not to wilt under her stare. "Long time, no see."

"I just saw you."

"No, I know—it was a joke." Oh God. "Because we saw each other at work, and now we're seeing each other again so soon after that." My cheeks feel warm. I clear my throat, trying to dislodge the embarrassment. "You called me Danielle," I blurt out.

Her eyebrows raise slightly. "That's your name."

"It's just that most people call me Dani—or they try to."

"Is that the name you prefer?"

"Oh God, no," I laugh awkwardly. "I've never liked the nickname."

"Ah."

This woman must think I'm an idiot. Would she fire me for how socially inept I'm being? "Doing some shopping?" I manage to ask.

Her eyebrows narrow almost imperceptibly. "Yes, that's why I'm here, at the store."

Christ, Danielle, get a grip. "Right. Well, it was nice seeing you—"

"You seemed to be admiring this specific section." She nods to the shelves in front of us.

Where I was just fondling a box of pasta.

My face is definitely beet red now. "I'm gluten free. For medical reasons, not by choice. Not that there's anything wrong with choosing that, I just didn't really have that choice. Anyway, I was just surprised with how many options this place has for me," I bumble on.

"And what is your medical reason?"

I blink. That feels highly personal for a near-stranger to ask, but I find my mouth saying, "Celiac Disease," before I can stop myself.

"Ah," she replies, as if absorbing this information.

My mouth keeps forming words. "Yeah. I was diagnosed a decade ago. Although, Jeremy seemed to struggle a lot with the change."

"Who?" she asks, her eyes nearly glowing in the fluorescent lighting.

Fuck. I shouldn't have said that. I shouldn't have brought him up. "Oh, just...an ex." I wave my hand dismissively. "It doesn't matter."

"This was your partner when you were diagnosed?" Her tone is slightly sharper now.

"Uh, yeah, I mean, he was my fiancée, but not anymore." I rush to get the words out. "He isn't in my life at all. I'm single." I can't stop blabbing. Shut up, shut up, shut up.

Blair's face remains nearly neutral, but I can sense... annoyance, maybe? Her shoulders have tightened slightly; the corners of her mouth have dropped just a hair.

She must be irritated with my ramblings. I clear my throat. "Sorry, I should let you get on with your shopping." I turn to my cart and say over my shoulder, "Nice to see you again, Blair," before I scurry down the aisle.

Well, so much for sticking it out at this new job. I need to find a new one now. I can't face Blair after having three awkward interactions with her.

I rush through the self-checkout, my mind running a mile a minute. I don't get why this random woman unnerves me so much. Maybe it's because I can sense her intelligence and confidence. She's definitely intimidating. If she wasn't, I probably wouldn't think twice about her. Bags in hand, I speed walk to my car, hoping to not have another run-in with Blair for a while.

Chapter 5
Blair

This woman is fascinating to me.

It's hard to come by others that I don't find dull or incredibly moronic. At times when I've been incredibly reckless, I've toyed with some that I found beneath me, like a child playing with her dolls.

But Danielle is different. The mask she wears is on too tightly. She acts like she's just a normal girl, but that's all it is–an act. She's just been conditioned to think this is how she should be.

She's one of us, the voice in my head chimes.

The darkness she has is kept locked away, ignored, malnourished. All it needs is to be let free.

And I'm the one who must do it.

Eyeing the gluten free section, I take a mental note of each item she was gawking at just a moment ago. Various types of flour–almond, rice, coconut, even banana, which sounds disgusting–sit on the shelves.

Without giving it a second thought, I place each kind into my cart.

I was twelve when I nearly killed my mother.

Controlling my impulses as a child was difficult, and I enjoyed manipulating certain peers. I had been caught snipping off a fellow child's ponytail in class, just to see how she would react. She had cried and tattled, landing me in the principal's office. I was suspended from school and sent home with my very angry mother, carrying a small Ariana on her hip. She grounded me for a month as punishment.

My mother wasn't a bad parent, necessarily. She was simply... unreliable. It was hard to know how she'd react to different situations, hard to predict. I'm not sure when I realized it; maybe I'd always known she was emotionally immature and not truly ready to be a parent. Regardless, we spent a lot of my childhood butting heads.

This was the first time she ever put her foot down, though. It wasn't like I had any friends or that being grounded barred me from any of my favorite activities, as I was a bit of a loner, but it was the sheer fact that she was telling me what to do. This woman who had no sense of boundaries or understanding of how to be a parent was telling *me* what to do?

I didn't like it. In fact, I hated it. I hated her. That's when I pictured it: I'd crush up a few of her sleeping pills and mix it into her nightly wine. She usually left the glass on the dining room table while she got little Ari ready for bed. I'd wait for the pills and wine to kick in. Then I'd smother her with her own pillow.

I went through with drugging her, and I nearly made it to placing the pillow over her face when I spotted Ari in her crib across the room. She was standing up, her little hands holding the bars of her crib, her eyes trained on me.

The potential consequences ran through my head in that moment: me getting caught, the both of us being sent away. If I went through with it, I never would see my half-sister again.

So, I stopped–and murdered someone else instead.

I would kill for my sister, but I have also stopped myself from doing so for her. Her husband is a loser and doesn't deserve her, but I know she'd be devastated if he wound up dead.

Now there's another person I'd kill for in my life. I doubt I'll stop myself the next time.

Chapter 6

This one picked me up in his car, as if he can't even bother to bed *me* in a proper bed.

He pulls into the forest preserve's small parking lot. As expected, it's empty.

Perfect.

"Hope this is okay," he offers as he puts the car in park. "It can be kinda romantic out here."

Uh huh. I look over and give him a grin. "Of course," I say, forcing my voice to sound sweet.

He smirks before his eyes dip to my chest, and he leans forward, eyes already closed.

I have no desire to touch him, but I make myself hinge towards him and press my lips to his. He starts moving his lips against mine, and truthfully, it's not bad. I expected way worse.

His large hands fumble to undo my seat belt. I pull back slightly, but he follows, capturing my mouth again. My eyes stay open as I watch those hands wind around my waist, attempting to pull me across the dashboard. Yeah, not really gonna work for me.

I slip my fingers into my coat pocket and palm the knife that's waiting for its time to shine.

Do it, the voice purrs. *Do the world a favor.*

"Come on over," he rasps against my lips. "I don't bite. Although, I could be convinced."

Gross. All right, that was it.

I reel back and pull the knife from my pocket, slamming it into his throat.

His eyes bulge as his hands go to the handle protruding from his neck. All he can do is make gurgling noises as he fumbles to pull it out.

I just sit back and wait. "You don't deserve to live after what you did to that girl. She was only sixteen. How old are you, like twenty-eight?" I scoff. "Pathetic."

He slumps back against his seat, the light slowly leaving his eyes as he tries to take a breath, but only short pants pass his lips.

I stare at him, making sure I'm the last thing he sees before he's greeted by death.

Chapter 7
Blair

It's shockingly easy to break into Danielle's home. She might as well have left the front door wide open.

I inspect the locking mechanism on her front door. It looks ancient. She'll need better security.

Don't want anyone breaking in.

I make quick work of the lock, hearing the satisfying *click* as it gives way. Pushing the door open, I peer in to see a dark living room. No sign of a pet I didn't know about. I step inside, placing the Ghostface mask I brought over my face. Costumes are currently on sale, and I don't need her knowing it's me. Not yet.

Ever since meeting her, I can't think of anything else. It's as if she's a siren, calling out to me, dragging me out to sea. The danger that lurks beneath her skin is intoxicating.

I've encountered others like me over the years, but none have made me feel like this. Mad. Obsessed. Desperate to know more. It's like she *could* be like me, but her mask is so tightly stuck to her face, she doesn't even know she's wearing it.

I need to help her uncover her full potential.

I slink across the floorboards towards the stairs. According to the Zillow profile of her home, the primary bedroom is on the second floor. I scoured any and all information I could find about her house, so I knew exactly where to find her. Waiting for her to go to bed felt like the longest wait of my life—I sat on my motorcycle down the street, fighting the urge to come in the second the lights went out.

The step creaks under my weight, making me freeze. My ears perk up, listening for any indication she's heard me.

Nothing.

I let out a silent breath and tiptoe the rest of the way up.

Some foreign sensation pulls me forward, as if a hook is embedded in my stomach and I'm being reeled in. Something in my chest squeezes. Is this what excitement feels like?

Gliding down the hall, I beeline it to her bedroom, where the door is ajar. Placing my palm upon the wood, I take a deep breath, steadying myself but not letting my mind tell me this is a terrible idea. A violation. A crime, no less.

None of that really matters. I need to know more.

I steel my spine and ease the door open.

There she is, fast asleep. Her hair is spread across her pillow, her eyes covered by an eye mask, and she has ear plugs in.

Dead to the world.

My feet guide me closer until I'm next to her bed. I watch her chest rise and fall with rapt attention. She has no idea what is in store for her.

My ogling is interrupted by her phone screen lighting up on the nightstand beside me.

I peer down at it. Twenty text messages and fifteen missed calls.

I pick the phone up and swipe to open it.

The demand for the Face ID pops up. I roll my eyes. Face ID isn't good security. What would happen if she's asleep and I simply place the phone over her? Then whoever wanted into her phone could easily do it.

Gripping the device in one hand, I gently push the eye mask onto her forehead, hovering the phone over her peaceful face.

It clicks and opens.

Her eyebrows bunch together, so I slowly ease the eye mask back in place before she turns onto her side, showing me her back.

I open her recent missed calls. They're all under an Unknown Caller ID.

Pressing the screen to open her voicemail, I see this Unknown Caller has left multiple voicemails, some as old as a few months ago. None of them have been listened to. Why is she keeping these?

I press play on the most recent one and hold the phone to my ear. A man's angry voice filters through.

"You better answer the phone, you stupid fucking bitch. You think you can just ignore me? You'll never get rid of me. I'll always find you, and I'll make your life a living hell."

I listen to the next one, then the next. All vitriol spewed at her, with increasing threats of violence.

Is this the ex she mentioned?

Anger spurs in my stomach, making me grip the phone tighter with each nasty word that comes out of his mouth. How dare he speak to her in such a way. I want to kill him. I want to cut him open, bit by bit, hearing his cries and pleas for mercy as I slice him apart.

After the fifth voicemail, I've had enough. I close out of her phone and place it back on the nightstand. As much as I'd love to delete them so she never has to hear such disgusting things said to her, it's best I don't—these blatant threats will be useful if she needs a restraining order.

Not that a restraining order will do much against someone like this.

A gentle sigh catches my attention just as she turns back over, splaying on her back. I stare down at her for a few minutes, taking in her even breathing. This man will never get close to her.

Which just shows how much she needs me. Once she lets the darkness out, she'll never have to deal with someone like that again. I'm the only one who can help her do this.

Besides, I love ridding the world of disgusting filth like that poor excuse of a man.

Leaning forward, I lightly caress her cheek with my finger.

Her skin is smooth and soft under my fingertip. "Don't worry," I whisper. "I'll help you."

Chapter 8
Danielle

"Two men have gone missing approximately a week apart. Police have yet to rule out if these cases are related," the news reporter on TV says.

I hum to myself as I finish making my breakfast, letting the news be background noise. I've survived my first week at my new job. Everyone is very *friendly*, which has already become annoying. I needed the entire weekend to sit around and do nothing just to recuperate.

My gluten-free bagel shoots up in the toaster as I hear a knock on my door.

"Huh. I didn't order anything," I say to Swim Shady, who flits about in his tank across the room. Padding over to the front door, I take a quick look through the peephole.

Two burly men stand on the other end.

My body freezes for a split second. Every time I see a man with the same build, panic shoots up my spine, worried it's him. Worried that he's finally found me.

Calm down, I tell myself. *It isn't Jeremy.*

I open the door just enough to pop my head through. "Hello. Can I help you?"

"Hi, ma'am. Are you—" the man looks down at the clipboard in his hands "Danielle Taylor?"

"Yes, that's me. What's this about?"

He raises his eyes. "We're here to install your new security system."

I blink. My what? I open the door a bit more and step into the opening. "I'm sorry, there must be some sort of mix-up. I didn't order a new security system."

The man furrows his bushy brows as he glances down at his clipboard again. "Danielle Taylor at 932 Monroe Street?"

"Yes," I say slowly. "That's me, but I didn't set this up."

The guy behind him looks down at his boots while the one in front looks back at me and shrugs. "Well, it's paid for already, ma'am. It's state of the art, too. Maybe a loved one thought you needed it."

My brain filters through everyone I know who might've done such a thing. The only people in my life that know the extent of Jeremy's abuse are my two friends from college, who took me in when I first left him. But why wouldn't they just tell me?

I shake my head. "Uh, if it's paid for...okay, great, go ahead."

He nods and says, "It won't take long. We'll just need an hour, and then we'll walk you through all the features."

I nod absently, distracted by this strange turn of events. I close the door and head into the kitchen, where I left my phone on the counter. Reaching for it, I pull up the only group chat I'm in.

BONG RIPPING BITCHES

Me: Okay, fess up. Who did it?

Kristina: ??

Lacy: I'm not sure what you're talking about, but it wasn't me!

Me: Who ordered me a "state of the art" security system for my new house?

Lacy: Oh, definitely wasn't me. You know I'm drowning in student loan debt atm

Kristina: Wasn't me, either. Maybe your mom?

I snort. My mom and I haven't spoken much since I called off the engagement. She was won over by Jeremy's charm, much like I was, but because she wasn't subjected to his violent tendencies, she thinks I just got cold feet. I decided it was best to go no contact—I couldn't stomach hearing about how I should try to get back together with that monster.

It was always shocking that she fell for Jeremy's tactics, considering my father was just like him. Although, I guess I didn't notice that until it was too late. I try not to blame her for making me feel abandoned by both choosing my shitty dad *and* my shitty ex, but it's hard not to. Every now and again, I'll feel guilty for basically ghosting my own mother and will reach out.

And I always regret it.

Still...maybe this is her way of showing that she wants to work on things. Closing out of the group chat, I call my mom before I can chicken out.

It rings once before she answers, "Danielle?"

"Hi, Mom."

"Oh, honey, it's so nice to hear from you." I hear rustling in the background. "I was just at Pilates and ran into Marianne Summers—you remember her? She's getting married to—"

"Yeah. Hey, Mom, I don't have a lot of time. I just wanted to ask if you bought a security system for my new house? The guys just showed up to install it."

A beat of silence. "I'm sorry, honey, but I didn't buy that for you. You haven't even told me where you're living, remember?" I can hear the bitterness in her voice. It makes my hackles rise. I couldn't trust her not to blab to Jeremy if he asked her, so I didn't tell her where I moved—just that I did, and that was that. She keeps going, "You know, Danielle, it really hurt my feelings when you just up and left, especially after calling off the wedding. Your Grandpa Jerry was hoping to see you in a wedding dress before he died."

I scoff. "Grandpa Jerry is only seventy and is perfectly healthy."

"Well, that's not the point." She sniffs. "I just don't know if it gets any better than Jeremy. Your father would have approved, bless his soul."

I've heard enough. I hang up without another word and turn my phone off. Part of me wants to tell her every terrible thing Jeremy did to me during our relationship. But, in my gut, I just don't think she'll believe me.

Sighing, I place my hands on the counter and hang my head. So, if my friends didn't do this, and my mother didn't do this...who did?

The technicians, Marty and Dan, walked me through my new fancy security system. It's like bank-level security:

porch cameras, motion sensor flood lights to illuminate the driveway and the backyard, a camera doorbell that will show video on both my phone and TV, and an alarm that will alert the police if the correct code isn't entered.

I hadn't considered getting this for myself, and I feel a bit stupid for not thinking of it.

And I feel on edge for not knowing where this came from.

Still, I'm going to use it. I feel safer already. Not that I really felt unsafe in this house before, but sometimes, I get paranoid he'll somehow find me and crash through the door.

Now, I'm rushing to get to work. I called my boss and told her that I'd be late, and she gave me a passive-aggressive response that it was fine but to get here quickly. I throw my bag into the passenger seat of my car and set my fancy new alarm system to 'Away' through the app.

Whoever bought this for me is going to get a massive kiss as thanks.

I peel out of my attached garage, feeling safe for the first time in a very long time.

By the time I make it into the office, I'm ushered into a meeting with the client. Everyone looks a bit frazzled as I sit down next to my coworkers.

"Ah, Danielle. Glad you could join us," Brian, the lead contact, greets me through the large television that shows everyone in their Zoom squares. "We were looking over these new specs and have concerns about the wording."

"Of course. What concerns do you have?"

"Well," he starts, "we have the statement, 'Vaping can damage your brain. Don't let vaping give you brain farts'."

I fight the urge to look around the room and shoot daggers at the creative team. I didn't approve that messaging as backed in research.

Brian looks at me through the screen. "We can't say that."

"Of course not," I agree. "I'll work with creative to make a better tagline. There are some promising findings about the connection between vaping and brain health, but obviously, brain farts are not a real thing." I can't help the subtle dig at whatever coworker was stupid enough to suggest it.

"Great," Brian responds. "We'd like to get the updated creative by next week. Is there anything else we need to discuss?"

"Actually, yes," I pipe up. "I found some fascinating research that links vaping with loss of taste and smell. Of course, we already knew this happened with smoking cigarettes, but it wasn't shown that vaping can do the same before."

"That's great, if you could..."

Suddenly, it feels like something is pulling me from my stomach. Like a rope is wrapped around me and someone is tugging me. I look away from the television and out into the office, my eyes immediately landing on Blair.

She doesn't just walk—she glides, like she's walking on water. Her dark, glossy hair is pulled back into an effortlessly chic bun, exposing her neck. She's wearing a navy button-down that makes her eerie eyes even more unsettling. Her gray trousers accentuate her tall frame, letting everyone know what she looks like while reminding us that no one can have her.

I gawk at her as she strides across the office, her expression reading as somewhat bored. She must feel me staring because her eyes catch mine. It's like watching a storm roll in after months of no rain.

She gives me a little grin. For some reason, it reads as a challenge.

Someone clears their throat next to me, and I snap out of it. The tugging sensation is gone, and I'm left back in the meeting I just mentally abandoned. Everyone is staring at me, as if waiting for me to say something. "Sounds good," I manage to get out, completely lost.

That seems to work for the client, though, as we say our goodbyes and they log off. As everyone gathers their things, I ask the woman next to me—Allison, I think— "Sorry, what did they say at the end? I totally missed it."

"Oh, they want a literature search for everything connecting vaping and loss of smell and taste," she says with a smile.

I sigh with relief. "Great, thanks."

"No worries. Wanna get lunch together? I'm starving."

"Oh, I bring my own. Thanks, though." *And I have no desire to spend time with you.*

She shrugs. "Well, maybe tomorrow."

"Yeah, sure," I answer, even though I won't really want to do that tomorrow, either.

As I follow Allison out of the conference room, I can't stop thinking about those odd stormy eyes.

Chapter 9
Blair

It's clear Danielle doesn't care for her coworkers.

I don't blame her, as the majority of these people are useless children who need constant guidance and reassurance. I don't care to spend much time in the office—not that I really need to. I started this agency with two college associates after struggling to work under other people's thumbs. We have all of the same qualities—charming when necessary, intelligent, and a basic lack of empathy—so we inherently understood one another.

Laura prefers to be in the office most days because she enjoys watching people squirm, and this is the perfect playground for her. Mark, on the other hand, hasn't once stepped foot in this building. I land somewhere in the middle.

That was exciting at first, but it's gotten stale. These workers don't provide enough stimulation for me anymore.

Until Danielle.

I watch her from afar, noting how she interacts with her colleagues. It's obvious to me that she thinks she's smarter than them—by her tone, the way she cuts them off once they begin to over-explain something. Granted, she *is* smarter than them.

She stirs her coffee with the small wooden stirrer absentmindedly after having yet another stilted conversation with a woman who was a bit too energetic for nine in the morning. Suddenly, she lets go of the stirrer, places the coffee on the counter, and speed walks out of the space. I follow silently, putting my hands in my trouser pockets as I prowl after her. She beelines it for the bathroom.

I should stop, but I can't—that hook embedded into my flesh is pulling me forward. I push open the bathroom door to find Danielle leaning over the sink with her head bowed. As the door shuts behind me, her head snaps up and our eyes lock.

We stand still for a few moments, unable to look away. Agitation and a calculating coolness swirls in her dark eyes—the same look I saw on Halloween.

Yes, I try to tell her. *I know exactly how it feels.*

But she breaks eye contact and straightens. Clearing her throat, she says, "Nice to see you yet again."

I lean my head back and look up at the ceiling. "It's difficult, isn't it? Having to work with people who are clearly below you."

She takes a second to respond. When I look back at her, her face is attempting to contort in confusion. "I'm not sure what you mean."

I give her a smirk. "You're intelligent, Danielle. I doubt you've been given enough work to keep you occupied."

"Oh." She fiddles with the buttons on her plaid dress. "Well, if there's any side work you'd like me to do, I'd be happy to get on it."

My smirk widens into a smile. "Wonderful. Stop by my office tomorrow and we'll discuss what I need from you." I don't wait for a response before forcing myself to turn and leave the bathroom.

I don't have any work for her to do—at least, not work that she thinks it'll be. I need more face-to-face time with her. More time together will, hopefully, let her see what life could be like if she tapped into her true nature.

And, if I'm honest, I want to be around her. She makes me feel things I've never felt before. When I met others like me, I never fixated on them or really cared what happened to them. If it was advantageous to have them around, then great. If it wasn't, I had no trouble distancing myself.

I don't know if I could distance myself from Danielle if things went south. My desire to help her has morphed into something else. Something dangerous, for both of us. But I won't stop watching her; I won't stop seeking her out. I'm headed down an unknown path, and I've never felt excited before now.

Chapter 10

Blair

I stand over Danielle's sleeping body, memorizing her breathing pattern, the way her mouth is slightly open. I ease her sleeping mask off to watch her eyes dart back and forth underneath their lids.

She's perfect. I want to keep her close, to devour her whole, so that no one else can have her. The urge to touch her overrides my brain as I slowly drag her duvet down her body. My mouth waters as my eyes skate over the exposed skin of her arms, her collarbones.

"Soon," I whisper to her. "Soon, I will have you."

Chapter 11
Blair

Danielle comes to my office the next morning with a pad of paper and a pen. "Good morning." She smiles at me, but it doesn't reach her eyes. She didn't sleep well last night.

When I slipped into her room, she was tossing and turning, mumbling in her sleep. It thwarted my plans to set cameras up throughout her home, as I can't have her waking up and catching me in the act.

Maybe I need to drug her.

I'm planning how to accomplish that as she sits in one of the chairs across from my desk. She squirms when I don't say anything. Heat floods my system.

"You mentioned you had work for me?" she prods.

I fight the urge to roll my eyes, wishing we didn't have to hide behind this facade. "I do." I lean back in my chair. "The client wants us to create anti-smoking marketing that will appeal to adults, but they also don't want us to market vapes as a cessation tool. I need you to look into whether vapes help someone quit smoking cigarettes."

She begins scribbling on her notepad. "Got it, yeah, I can do that." She pauses her writing and purses her lips. "I'm going to assume the client wants to steer away from vapes for cessation because the research is still so new—we don't really know the long-term effects of them yet." I'm not clear on if she's talking to me or to herself, but I hum noncommittally. It causes her to look back up at me.

I feel like I'm being sucked into her dark eyes, like they're a bottomless pool that I will happily drown in. I didn't see her as conventionally attractive, but she's definitely beautiful. Her curly hair frames her face, showing off her silky skin. The dimple on her right cheek peeks out just enough. My fingers twitch, desperate to caress her again.

Her breath hitches and her neck reddens. "Um, okay, yeah so I can definitely look into this for you." Her voice is husky, making me want to lunge at her from across the desk. "Do you need it by a specific date?"

"Yes," I lie, my voice sounding smooth, which is impressive considering what I'm fantasizing about. "I need something written up by tomorrow."

Her eyes nearly pop out of her head. "Oh, well, I have a lot to do this week—"

Here we go. I give her a condescending smile to push her buttons. I need to see how quick she is to anger—it's the easiest emotion for us to feel. We tend to escalate quickly and tear everything down with it.

"No," I interrupt. "I need it tomorrow."

Danielle furrows her eyebrows as her eyes narrow in agitation. "But—"

"I'll expect it on my desk by end of day tomorrow." Another strange sensation sits in my bones. I think I feel...giddy. Excited to see how she'll react.

But instead of responding with anger, her features smooth out, her face now carefully blank. "Not a problem."

Huh. Maybe she has a tighter leash on her rage than I thought. I have to figure out how to cut it loose.

"That's all," I tell her, waving my hand dismissively.

She swallows hard, as if shoving her emotions down, before giving me a bland smile and leaving my office.

Chapter 12

Danielle

I'm pissed off.

Blair's demand has completely derailed my week. I had several other things to do, but now I must drop everything for her. Luckily, my coworkers need no further explanation as to why I need more time on their projects than 'Blair needs me'.

It's obvious she unnerves them, but I get the sense that she makes them uncomfortable in a different way than she makes me uncomfortable. She makes me feel like she's stripped me bare every time she looks at me. Like she's staring into my soul.

Regardless, I'm mad. I nearly lost my cool in her office. It took nearly all of my self-restraint not to get angry.

But now that I'm back at my laptop, I type a bit more aggressively than necessary.

The next day, I knock on Blair's office door, ready to hand over my summary of what I found. Other countries have marketed vapes as a cessation tool for adults looking to quit smoking cigarettes, so it can be done here, if the client is open to changing their mind.

"Come in," Blair calls, so I step into her huge office.

She's leaning her ass against the front of her desk with her arms crossed. "What do you need, Danielle?"

My name on her tongue makes me shiver. "Um, hi. I just have the report you asked for?"

She cocks her head. "Report?"

I blink as I walk over, extending the printed summary page I hold in my hand. "About vapes as a cessation tool?"

"Ah." She reaches forward and takes it from me, her fingers gently brushing against mine. It feels like I've been zapped with raw energy.

Until she takes the report and flippantly tosses it onto her desk.

Anger ignites in my stomach. "I thought you needed it quickly because the clients needed it?"

"You assumed that," she chides. "Besides, I'm not sure what relevance my meeting with the client has on your work."

My mouth pops open, and I jam it closed immediately. Is she fucking serious? I'm now behind on a bunch of work because she needed this.

Don't freak out, don't freak out—

I force a smile onto my face. "Oh, well, I guess that's my mistake." My tone drips with sarcasm, but I can't quite bring myself to care. "Well, goodnight, Blair."

I spin on my heel and rush to the door before I do something I regret.

"If I have concerns about your work, how would you like to receive constructive feedback?"

Her question makes me pause. I turn around, not quite believing what I heard. "Excuse me?"

Amusement dances in her gray eyes, which surprises me. Is she laughing at me? "You finished this so quickly; if it's not thorough, I want you to know."

I let out a little laugh. "Believe me, I'm meticulous with my work."

She gives me a look of disbelief, which makes me see red. "I'll call you to my office, then, if I require revisions."

"Sure," I grit out.

I don't wait to be dismissed, nearly running out of the office before I punch her square in the face. I walk down the hall and rush into the bathroom, my anger making me feel like I'm having a hot flash. I reach the sink and dab cold water on my face, my neck.

She's an asshole.

Unfortunately, that asshole holds my job in her hands. I can't believe I felt...well, I'm not sure what I felt for her, exactly. She's obviously attractive, but she gives off dangerous energy. I feel like she'll suck me in and won't let me go if I get too close.

My phone buzzes in my pocket. It's probably Jeremy, calling from an unknown number to berate me again.

After a few deep breaths, my anger dissipates and I leave the bathroom, ignoring my phone.

I can deal with this. I can deal with her.

Chapter 13
Blair

The security system seems to be working perfectly.

I'm glad I made the investment. Now it's time to set up a system of my own.

I step onto Danielle's porch, already having disabled the flood lights and alarm system to avoid detection. Slipping my mask into place, just in case, I slink into the house.

The security system was for her, but these internal cameras are for me.

I sneak upstairs to check on her, finding her asleep. She seems to be quite a deep sleeper, when she finally finds it.

I make quick work of the hidden cameras in her room, pointing to her door and to her bed before heading downstairs, setting a camera in each room.

She was angry with me today. Good. That's entirely the point. I want to push her buttons, to see what she's capable of when she's up against a wall.

It'll take a lot of deprogramming, but I bet it will be beautiful.

The final hidden camera is now set up in her kitchen. I pass by a fish tank on my way and see a small fish staring at me. I pull my mask to the top of my head and stop and lean down so we're eye-to-eye. "Hello. Who are you?"

The fish opens and closes its mouth, obviously thinking I'll provide it with food. "You're not a very good guard dog," I inform it before straightening and looking around for what it wants. "But you're not a snitch either, and I respect that."

I grab the fish food that sits next to the tank and sprinkle some through the small opening in the tank's lid. It swims eagerly upwards, devouring the treat quickly.

I chuckle quietly and secure my mask back in place before leaving. I have much more in store for Danielle.

Chapter 14
Danielle

The rest of the work week passes by with no interruptions from Blair. I had enough work to deal with, especially after she forced me to move things around for her. And Jeremy has been blowing me up constantly. I never answer, which enrages him.

Today I got fifty calls. I had to turn my phone off eventually.

I'm pondering changing my phone number yet again as I drive up to my house and notice a reusable shopping bag on my front porch.

Pulling into my driveway, I shut my car off and walk to the door, unsure of what this is. I didn't order grocery delivery.

Standing over it, I bend down a bit to look inside. There's something that looks homemade inside—a circular pan with tin foil covering the top. I straighten and pull up my security app.

Rewinding through the day, I see me drive away, heading to work, but then nothing else until it shows me drive up and now standing here, staring at my phone. I shake my head. That's not right. Someone obviously left this here today.

I let out a huff of frustration and pick the bag up, unlock my front door, and head to the kitchen. Dropping the bag on the counter, I pull up the security footage again, my brows narrowing in concentration.

The footage is the same: just me leaving, then me coming home nine hours later. No sign of anyone.

"What the fuck," I whisper to myself, rewinding another time, as if the footage will magically change.

It's on the third replay when I notice it.

The leaves I don't want to rake on my front lawn get picked up by a gust of wind, throwing them across the walkway at nine this morning. But then, thirty minutes later, the walkway is clear. Then those leaves are picked up by the wind and splay over the concrete.

My breath catches in my throat. The footage has been tampered with. Whoever dropped this off managed to hack into the cameras and erase themselves from the feed so I wouldn't see them.

I put my phone down and look in the bag, my eyes snagging on an envelope next to the pan.

Reaching in, I lift the pan out and place it on the marble, then quickly grab the envelope. I rip it open with more force than necessary.

A note and a Polaroid are inside.

I've never worked with these materials, but I'm learning for you. From your secret admirer.

My blood goes cold. I shift my attention to the Polaroid. I have to squint to make out the contents, but it looks like a countertop with various gluten free flours laid out.

I turn my attention to the pan and rip the tinfoil off.

Cinnamon rolls greet me.

This person must be trying to tell me that they made gluten free cinnamon rolls. For me.

My mouth goes slack. Is this the same person that paid for the security system? It would make sense; how else would they know how to edit the camera footage?

Without thinking twice, I lift the pan, walk it over to my garbage can, and throw the entire thing in. No way am I eating something made by a stalker.

The word clangs through me. Stalker. Is that what this is?

It can't be…it can't be Jeremy. He would never do this. No, he would have probably just shown up here instead of going through the trouble of making something like this.

No, this is someone else entirely.

I rush around the house, locking the doors and shutting the curtains before running upstairs and basically barricading myself in my room. I push my desk against my door and stack a few things on top. There's no way anyone is getting through that. Luckily, my bathroom is attached to my room, so there's no need to leave until morning.

I head into the bathroom and turn on my shower, hoping to get rid of the unease worming around under my skin. Stripping off my clothes, I step into the scalding hot water, letting it distract me.

I can't shake the feeling, though, that I'm being watched. I know it's irrational, but it feels like someone is standing in here with me.

The feeling grows the longer I'm in here, so I quickly shut the water off, wrap myself in a towel, and head to my bed. I open the security app on my phone and stare at the screen.

No one out there, no signs of moments being rewound. A relieved sigh passes my lips. I'm alone—at least for now.

Chapter 15
Blair

I peer into the garbage and see the cinnamon rolls I made her and smile down at them.

Smart girl. She shouldn't eat something made by a stranger, even if I followed all necessary precautions for her autoimmune disease.

I'll make them for her again, where she can watch me like a hawk to ensure they're safe for her. I'd never want to hurt her.

At least, not like that.

I watched her trap herself in her room. My gift must have really spooked her. Sighing, I sit at her kitchen island, debating how far I should push her tonight.

Break down her bedroom door, the voice in my head demands. I thrum my fingers against the kitchen counter, considering it, wondering how she'd react.

"What do you think I should do?" I ask her little fish, who is staring at me through the glass. "I don't want to scare your mother *too* much."

His mouth opens and closes, as if we're having a conversation.

"You're right," I sigh. "It would be excessive tonight. Putting that tracker on her car tonight will have to do."

Reluctantly, I trudge to the door like a petulant teenager. I don't want to be away from her, but pushing her too hard won't help my case.

I slip into the darkness of her front porch. Walking to my motorcycle parked a block away, I decide I'll be back tomorrow. I need to see her again, even if it's just for a moment. Maybe she'll calm down and realize barricading her door is pointless.

As if that will deter me again.

Chapter 16
Danielle

A breeze caresses my body, making my nipples pebble. I shift, seeking the warmth of my blankets, but something firmer circles my breasts.

My brows furrow as I realize I'm not dreaming. I rip my eye mask off, and my eyes fly open to see two gloved hands feeling me up.

I gasp, and scurry to the other side of the bed, snatching a blanket to cover me. "What the fuck!" I screech.

Before me stands a tall frame, donned in all black, their face covered by a Ghostface mask.

My heart hammers in my chest, panic gripping me, making my eyesight cloud.

"What do you want from me?" My voice shakes. "If you want money—"

A low rumble comes from them. It takes me a moment to realize it's a laugh.

"Okay, no money," I whisper. "Um, I don't have anything valuable..."

"No."

I'm knocked from my panic for a split second.

Their voice is rough, but it's definitely a woman's voice.

Despite the situation, my body feels a bit of...relief.

A man stalking me and watching me while I sleep? Terrifying. But a woman doing it? Now that makes me feel *slightly* less horrified.

"Then what do you want?" I ask, voice coming out stronger now.

She tilts her head, as if studying me, although it's hard to tell with the mask. Then, without another word, she turns and strides out of the room, leaving me more confused than before.

I was too wired to sleep. Luckily, it's Saturday, so I don't have to drag my ass into work with only a few hours of sleep.

Someone was here in my house while I was sleeping.

After they left, I canvassed the entire house, worried they were hiding somewhere. There was no sign of anyone. In fact, there was no sign of forced entry at all; my front and back doors were locked, and they don't appear damaged in any way.

I don't even know what to do. The rational part of my brain is trying to turn on, but my adrenaline pumps too hard for any of my thoughts to stick. What does anyone do in situations like this? The police won't be of any help. I don't have any friends or family living close by.

Is that why she picked me, because I'm alone here?

I sit down at my desk, my body thrumming with energy as I pull open the drawer. Rummaging through the contents, I find a notepad and a pen. I slap them onto the wood and scribble **POTENTIAL STALKER LIST** onto the page.

"Okay, so what do I know?" I murmur to myself. "I know my stalker is a woman, and that she's tall—probably like six feet." I write those towards the top.

I wrack my brain for tall women I've interacted with recently.

"There was a tall woman at Target I spoke to a few weeks ago," I muse, and write down *TALL TARGET LADY?* on the paper. "Then there was the dental hygienist that I could've sworn was flirting with me..." I add her to the list.

Sighing, I sink into my desk chair, swiveling back and forth as I try to come up with other names. Maybe that one coworker who has been really nice to me. I think her name's Allison. She works closely with the federal contract, so we've been sitting close to one another in the office. I've brushed off her invitations to lunch more than a few times. Is she the kind of woman who'd take offense to something so small? I jot her name down.

I tap my pen on the notepad impatiently, trying to think of who else would be deranged enough to do something like this.

Suddenly, a light bulb goes on in my head.

The woman from trick-or-treating. The same one who happens to basically own the agency I work for. Who I ran into at the store, and the one that seemingly enjoys irritating me.

Blair.

Every time I'm near her, I feel a pull to her. I can't describe it—it's as if it's happening on a molecular level.

Did she order the security system? Did she leave the food on my doorstep? It has to be her.

The security system was expensive. I ran into Blair at the grocery store, in front of the gluten free section. She knows where I live, what I can and can't eat.

I swallow hard, my hand shaking as I write her down. The little voice in my head is telling me I'm right.

Conflicting feelings flow through me, warring with each other. I should be disgusted, freaked out, angry. But it's mixed with a feeling of...warmth.

I'm sick, I think to myself, shaking my head before throwing the notepad back into the desk haphazardly and standing up. I head downstairs and out to my attached garage. I need to clear my head, and a walk always works.

There's a beautiful cemetery about a few miles away that's the perfect spot. I rip open the garage door and storm to my car, throwing myself into the driver's side.

Placing my hands on the steering wheel, I take a few deep breaths, trying to calm my body. I close my eyes and breathe and breathe and breathe.

Eventually, my heart stops skipping beats and my hands no longer feel clammy. I lift my hand to the garage door opener clipped to my sun visor and peel out, needing this to wipe the feeling of her hands on me.

And the conflicting feelings that creates.

Chapter 17
Blair

I turn over and grab my phone from the nightstand—I couldn't sleep anyway. Not after being caught in the act.

Opening the security app, I see Danielle's car pull out of her driveway. It's five in the morning. Where is she going? Is she going to the police?

A little thrill goes down my spine at the thought. They wouldn't do anything for her. She has no evidence and no idea that it's me. Although, after last night, she might—if she could recognize my voice.

I track her car with rapt attention as she zig-zags through town, watching the little dot move along my screen. After a few minutes, she stops at a cemetery.

Interesting. Yet another example of how Danielle is wearing a mask—if she was truly afraid of me, she wouldn't be driving to a cemetery, now would she? She'd be a panicking, sobbing mess at the thought of someone doing this to her.

The urge to go to her home drives me from bed, throwing my clothes on. I'm not even sure why I want to—she isn't there. Maybe it's something about being in her space. Or maybe I want to see what she'll do when she finds out I can come into her home, her life, whenever I please.

I waste no time making my way to her house, prowling up the front steps as if I own the place. I don't bother meddling with the security footage; I want her to know I was here, although I just keep my hood up to obscure my face. Don't want the neighbors raising any alarms to someone in a mask entering her house.

Pushing through the front door, I beeline for her bedroom, letting my instincts guide me.

Her bedroom is in disarray, with her sheets rumpled, clothes strewn across nearly every surface, and pens littering the floor by her desk. Her e-reader sits on her desk, plugged into its charger. I tap the screen, and it lights up, showing me what she's currently reading. I lean down and my eyebrows raise.

I'm spiraling out of control as he slams into me, over and over. "Thank you, Daddy," I cry. The ropes push into my skin, burning deliciously.

"That's a good girl, baby," he grunts, his cock splitting me in half.

"Oh my," I chuckle, skimming through before swiping out of this book and into her library.

Erotica title after erotica title, showing covers of shirtless men, women kissing, and a few that seem to feature a half-human, half-octopus. I open one and flip through the contents, finding nothing but kinky scenes depicted on the pages.

If this is what she's reading, I wonder how likely it is that she'll want to try these things.

Oh, this is going to be fun.

I lock the e-reader, my mind logging every sexual encounter for future use.

That's when I see it: her desk drawer slightly ajar.

I ease it open. It looks as if she pulled out this notepad but was haphazard in putting it back. The corner got stuck, keeping the drawer from fully closing. I sit myself down at her desk and scan the note she scribbled out.

POTENTIAL STALKER LIST

TALL TARGET LADY?

DENTAL HYGIENIST

ALLISON

<u>BLAIR</u>

I grin when I see my name. Seems like Danielle has figured it out—or has *nearly* figured it out. If she really thought it was me, she wouldn't be dilly-dallying at some cemetery.

No, if she's like me the way I know she is, she'd be trying to hunt me down.

I place the notepad back in the drawer and stand before peeking around her room, desperate to stay here forever. I envision sleeping here, with her warm, soft skin touching mine as we wake each morning. How it would feel to caress her, squeeze her, hold her down as I have my way with her.

Before I even register what I'm doing, I'm crawling into her bed, throwing her duvet over me. I lay face down, burying my face into her pillow and taking a deep inhale. My mouth waters as lavender and vanilla flood my nose. A ravenous hunger overcomes me, a deep, aching sensation that I don't think I'll ever satiate.

With a soft groan, I picture Danielle spread out on this bed, her legs open as she plays with herself. God, even to watch her pleasure herself would bring me to my knees.

I've always loved to watch, but I have a feeling that watching Danielle come undone would destroy me.

I waste no time; my fingers dip under my waistband towards the wetness already between my legs. I grind my hips against my hand, letting myself get lost in my imagination and her scent still in my nose. My face stays firmly pressed against her pillow—I might suffocate and die here for Danielle to find my body, but it would be worth it.

My mind runs away with the little scenes I just read as I gyrate my hips, picturing Danielle and myself acting them out. Danielle's face soft with pleasure as I taste her; her crying out my name as I edge her, again and again, until tears stream down her cheeks; her trembling under me as I split her open with a dildo.

I flip over and shuck off my boots and pants, still riding the high as my finger roughly circles my clit. Arousal builds quickly as I flit through all the ways I want Danielle. I want her begging for me, to have her cry—and to maybe hurt a little. To fight back, even when she knows it's pointless to do so.

Turning my head, I bury my face into her pillow and take another deep inhale. A moan escapes my lips as her scent overwhelms me and throws me over the edge. Release sparks throughout my body, making me writhe in Danielle's bed. I want her here so she can see what she does to me. What even picturing her makes me feel.

As I come down from the high, I rub my cheek on her pillow, hoping my own scent will mar it. Hopefully she'll like how I smell, how I taste.

Slowly, I untangle myself from the bed, standing in her room with my pants still off. I look behind me at the mattress and notice a prominent wet spot I left behind.

It makes me smile. A little sign that I was here. *It's like a love note, in a way,* I think as I reluctantly put my pants back on. I pull my phone from my pocket and check Danielle's location.

Looks like she's on her way back home.

My stomach feels uneasy at leaving, as if my body is fighting my decision. "I'll be back," I promise myself. It's not like I can be away from her for long anyway.

No one has ever impacted me like this. But Danielle...for some reason, she's a completely different story.

I pull my hood up so her cameras can't register my face as I saunter down the street to my bike. I don't think I could leave her alone if I tried. Not that I want to, of course. It's too late for that.

I'll go back tonight, I decide as I climb onto my motorcycle. Just because I can and because I want to.

And maybe because being away from her is starting to feel impossible.

Chapter 18
Danielle

The entire day has dragged on, my mind struggling to focus on any task long enough to distract me from waking up to a person fondling me. I bustle around the house, throwing myself into deep cleaning, but Blair's face keeps popping up. It's like she's taunting me.

I own you, I can almost hear the smirk in her voice. *I own you and there's nothing you can do. I own you and you'll learn to love it.*

It just makes me scrub my kitchen sink more aggressively.

I've decided that my only option is to confront her. I know that every movie makes it clear a person should *not* do this, but this is real life. There has to be some rational part of her, somewhere deep down—she's a partner of a prestigious marketing firm, for crying out loud. She had to rise through the ranks and be successful enough to become a partner. She wouldn't be successful if she was completely unhinged, would she?

After frantically cleaning my house, I drag myself upstairs and into the bathroom. I turn the stream on and quickly hop in, sliding the shower door shut and letting the water wash away the sterile smell of cleaning products.

My mind seems incapable of thinking about anything but Blair. I know I should be scared, but all I feel is aggravated that this is happening to me. I moved here for a fresh start, and that does *not* include someone stalking me.

Why me? Is there something about me that makes me an easy target for abusers and psychos? I used to struggle with people-pleasing—maybe they sense I could easily fall into that pattern again?

Something else blends with my annoyance, and I'm struggling to get rid of it.

I need to calm down.

My eyes focus on my detachable shower head. Maybe an orgasm will help me relax—and help me think about something else for a minute.

I reach up and grab my shower head, the hot water spraying me as I position it between my legs. The steady beat of the water hits my clit, working me up. I close my eyes and imagine the two women from the erotica novel I recently read.

One is a CEO and the other is her employee—

I shake my head, trying to get rid of the image. Nope, not that one. Too close to real life. Sighing, I think about the one where the man breaks into this woman's home and—

Fuck, what is wrong with me? I grit my teeth and force myself to imagine the monster romance I just read. Blair may be a monster, but she doesn't have tentacles.

I close my eyes and settle into my fantasies, letting the imagery of the tentacles pinning me down fill my mind. *"Pathetic, little human,"* the creature sneers as I try to wrestle free. *"You're mine now."*

A whimper escapes my lips as arousal floods me. The shower stream hits me just right, just enough.

In my mind, more tentacles wrap around me, gagging me. I fight against them but don't really want to get away.

"You're mine," the creature repeats, but its voice sounds familiar. *"I'm never going to let you go."*

Suddenly, Blair is in my fantasy; the monster is gone and all that holds me down are ropes. Her body is on full display, and it makes me moan.

Fuck it, thinking of Blair *one time* is fine. It doesn't have to mean anything. Besides, I really want to come.

My orgasm starts to build as I picture her grinding on me, pressing herself against me and using my body for her pleasure. Her sinful mouth is everywhere, lapping at my neck, my nipples, my clit. She's ravenous for me, and I can't get enough.

"Fuck," I whisper aloud.

Release spirals out of control, too quickly for me to hold back. I come with Blair's name on my lips, my body contracting with pleasure as the water pushes me to my breaking point. I don't care what I thought about to get here; all that matters is the overwhelming sensations that rip me apart.

My body feels lighter as I put the shower head back in place and shut off the water, even if I feel a bit of shame at what I just fantasized. Stalking isn't hot, no matter what my books say.

"Get yourself together," I mumble. "She'll be back, and I need to be ready."

I towel off and slip on my pajamas, anxiety sitting in my stomach. This is a terrible idea, but there are no other options.

I need to confront her.

Chapter 19
Blair

I watch Danielle from the doorway as she brings herself to orgasm, my name spilling from her lips.

She wants me.

My skin prickles as I watch her head lean back, eyes closed, grinding against the water from her shower. I need to have her.

She's going to be mine and I'm never letting her go.

I knew I was right in wanting her.

She comes down from her high, placing the shower head back and turning off the water. I retreat silently into her dark bedroom as she steps out of the shower. This obsession has become something greater, something far more dangerous. It's like a sickness that infiltrated every cell, fusing with my very DNA, taking over everything I am.

I back into the hallway and head downstairs as I wait for her to go to bed. My heart is beating so loudly, I'm surprised she can't hear it. Gliding into the kitchen, I find myself in front of her fish tank again. For some reason, this little fish has left an impression on me. Maybe because he acts as a companion to me as I wait for my time with Danielle.

He swims to the glass and stares at me, waiting for me to feed him. With a silent laugh, I grab his food and sprinkle some in.

"Soon," I whisper, "your mother and I will be together all the time, and she'll realize you're getting double the meals."

He doesn't seem to care as he flits from one piece of food to the next.

I lean against the counter, rifling through my backpack for my sketchbook. As soon as I open it, my pen is flying across the page, depicting what I just witnessed as I wait for Danielle to fall asleep.

Chapter 20
Danielle

I pretend to be asleep, waiting for her to arrive.

My stalker.

I know I'm playing with fire. Someone who is willing to break into my house while I'm sleeping is dangerous.

My hand slips under my pillow, feeling the handle of the knife I stashed under there. If she tries anything, I'm not afraid to use it. I didn't survive an abusive relationship just to be murdered like *this*.

I burrow under the blankets, hoping my fake sleep act is convincing. I'm wearing my sleep mask and my ear plugs to make it seem believable—while I hate stifling those senses, she'll notice if they're missing.

Time moves at a snail's pace. Five hours could have passed, or five minutes, I have no idea. I fight with myself to breathe evenly, to not rip out my ear plugs just so I can fixate on every creak that moves through the house.

I'm like a live wire, ready to snap, when I *feel* her presence. It's as if the air in the room has become charged. Even though I can't see or hear, I can sense that she's nearby.

I take deep breaths, working to relax my body, even though all I want to do is bolt upright and shriek like a banshee.

Slowly, the blanket is pulled back, revealing my face, my shoulders, until she stops at my stomach.

Don't freak out, don't freak out, don't—

A feather light touch floats across my cheek, once, twice, a third time before I reach my limit. I rip my eye mask off and pull the knife from under my pillow. Rushing into a seated position, I scream, "*What the fuck are you doing?*"

She backs away slowly, but she doesn't seem frightened or startled. She shoves her hands into her pant pockets, her shoulders relaxed. Blair stops at the end of the bed and cocks her masked head.

I scramble for the ear plugs, ripping them out so quickly it upsets my ear canals. Her calmness worries me.

Waving the knife in the air, I shriek, "Did you not hear me? I *said* what the *fuck* are you doing?!"

Silence.

My heart hammers in my chest and I'm nearly hyperventilating. "Why are you in my house? Why are you watching me while I sleep and dropping off gifts?"

Nothing.

I'm pretty sure my blood pressure is skyrocketing. "Answer me!"

"You asked me multiple questions. For which are you expecting a response?"

My mouth falls open. "All of them, you psycho."

"That's an offensive term."

"You're offending *me* by showing up in my bedroom wearing a Halloween mask!"

It sounds like she sighs, although it's muffled, as if she's exasperated.

"Well?" I push. "What are you doing?"

"I'm watching you."

"No shit," I snarl. "Why?" "Because I want to."

Her answer knocks me stupid. "You—what? You can't just—"

She crosses her arms. "I can do whatever I please."

My mouth hangs open. "No. No, you can't. You can't break into someone's house and watch them sleep. It's illegal. And very, very creepy." My entire body feels like it's ready to ignite the second she even thinks about coming closer. "Who are you?" I ask, dread sitting in my stomach.

She taps her pointer finger on her bicep a few times before answering, "Do you really want to know?"

Yes. No. "I don't know," I blurt out.

Her chuckle makes a shiver run down my spine. "You already know who I am."

My stomach nearly drops out of my ass.

"Blair." My voice is strained, barely above a whisper.

She doesn't say anything, leaving me to nearly become overwhelmed by my racing thoughts.

I love being right, but I hate what I'm right about in this instance.

My stalker owns me—or rather, owns the company I work for.

There's nothing I can do. No one will ever believe a partner is stalking their new employee. I'll have to find a new job, maybe even move again.

Red-hot agitation fills my veins. "Get the fuck out," I growl at her, "and don't ever come back. Don't even *look* at me again."

"Oh, this doesn't work like that, Danielle." She uncrosses her arms and hinges forward, pressing her palms into the mattress. "You're mine, and I have no desire to let you go."

"I'm serious. Get out of my house. I never want to see you again."

She shakes her head, as if she's dealing with a petulant child. "There's so much you need to learn."

Her words confuse me enough to pause my anger. Before I can demand what the hell that's supposed to mean, she pushes off the bed, turns, and leaves my room. I listen to her strut through my house, and then the front door open and close.

I dart from my bed with my knife, not trusting for a second it was *that* easy to get her to leave. I hold the knife in both hands, outstretched, as I creep down my stairs.

No sign of her.

I check every room and rip open every door, but I don't find her. It isn't until I've searched in my coat closet that I feel relief.

My hands shake from the adrenaline, so I drop the knife onto my coffee table and sit on the couch. I take deep breaths to regulate my nervous system after what just happened. My breaths end up being more like gasps, but eventually, my body slumps against my couch, worn out. All five senses start to come back online, letting me experience my living room normally again.

Sighing, I look down at my knife. What was I really going to do with that thing? It pains me to admit it, but I don't think I would have hurt her.

The thought makes me annoyed with myself. She deserves to be stabbed for what she's done.

Then, something under one of my coasters catches my eye.

Tentatively, I reach forward, brushing my fingers along what feels like a piece of paper. I lift the coaster to find a note that looks very similar to the stationary I have in my desk.

I unfold the piece of paper to find my potential stalker list.

Hands shaking, I spread it out against the coffee table and notice handwriting that isn't mine.

Blair's name is circled, and underneath, reads:

Well done.

I'll see you soon.

Emotions run through me, too quickly to recognize them all. I rip the list into shreds, not ready to even con-sider whether her words are a promise or a threat.

Chapter 21
Danielle

I pull my car into my doctor's parking lot, frazzled at being late. My gynecology appointment was scheduled to begin seven minutes ago.

I've been struggling to sleep ever since Blair crashed into my life. Her words bounce around in my head on a loop.

There's so much you need to learn.

Learn about what? Why she's stalking me? I don't really need to know why—I just need her to stop.

A strange sensation sits in my stomach when I think of this sick game ending. I refuse to acknowledge it—if I do that, it'll make the feeling real.

I haven't seen her at work since, which makes me feel...weird. When I asked a coworker about it, he told me, "Blair comes and goes a lot. I've honestly been surprised at how often she's been in the office lately."

Has she been coming there to see me? I almost can't believe the little thrill that goes down my spine at that thought.

There's been no activity on my security cameras, either. I rigged my bedroom door to drop a bucket of cold water on her if she tried creeping on me again. It made me feel like I was in *Home Alone*, but I refused to feel silly—I need sleep, and if she broke in, this would alert me to her without having to stay up every night.

But there's been no sign of her.

I should be relieved, but I'm not. And I hate that.

Rushing into the doctor's office, I try to push everything from my mind. I tell the receptionist my name and fill out the paperwork quickly, my penmanship looking near illegible in my haste.

Until one question gives me pause.

Do you feel safe at home?

I used to hover my pen over this question, debating if I should answer it honestly. Yes, I was very unsafe at home, but I was too afraid of what would happen if I told the truth. Would they report it somehow? Would he find out? I was terrified of what he'd do to me if he knew I told anyone.

So, I'd answer yes.

It feels odd to say yes this time, too. I am very clearly *not* safe at home—I have someone literally breaking in whenever she pleases.

For some reason, I mark yes again. It doesn't make me feel disappointed like it has in the past. I feel...relieved.

Sighing, I hand my paperwork to the front desk and sit in the empty waiting room. The only logical explanation for this reaction is that I'm a fucked-up individual.

At some level, I must not be afraid of Blair. If I was, I'd have taken real action to get her to stop—reported her to a hotline or something. I'd never call the cops about it; I learned the lesson that cops never take victims seriously the hard way.

She hasn't threatened to hurt me.

She makes me feel...things.

Yeah, I'm definitely fucked up to rationalize her behavior.

A nurse calls my name, snapping me from my thoughts. I gather myself and rush after her. We go through the clinic until we reach a patient room. After recounting my health history, she leaves me to get undressed from the waist down.

I strip my leggings and underwear off, covering my underwear—my doctor can check me out downstairs, but I draw the line at her seeing my floral bikini panties.

I get myself situated on the patient table, wrapping the crinkly paper over me. My eyes float around the room until my attention snags on a poster about the stages of pregnancy.

I'm startled by the doctor knocking on the door before stepping into the room, already mid-sentence. "Hi there, I'm Doctor Sullivan." She gives me a smile before walking over to the sink to wash her hands. "You're here for a routine pap smear, correct?"

"That's right," I tell her.

"Any issues? Abnormal paps in the past?"

"I had one abnormal pap when I was twenty-one."

"And what were the results?" she probes, taking some paper towels from the dispenser, drying her hands before shutting the water off.

I think back to my first pap smear. It was a harrowing experience. "They said I had HPV, and needed to get a pap smear every year. I got one three years ago that came back normal, so then they told me to only get one every three years."

Doctor Sullivan nods as she puts her gloves on. "Got it. Did you get the Gardasil shots as a child?"

"Yep."

"Well," she says as she sits on the stool in front of me, "It sounds like your body managed to get rid of the HPV on its own, which is good. We'll do a pap today and see if it comes back abnormal. Would you like to do STI testing today, too?"

Should I? I got tested a few months before Jeremy and I broke up because I could just tell something down there was...off. I came back positive for chlamydia, but I never slept with anyone besides him.

Which meant he'd cheated on me.

It had really been my final straw. He was going to cheat on me after subjecting me to his cruelty?

"No, that's okay." I shrug, trying to control the shame leaking through my skin. There's nothing shameful about chlamydia, but thinking about him fucking other people while he was with me always makes me sick.

She nods. "Well, go ahead and scoot down—"

A knock on the door makes us both pause and turn to look.

A moment passes, and in waltzes Blair.

My mouth drops open.

"Sorry I'm late, darling," she croons to me, shutting the door before coming over and placing a chaste kiss to my cheek. My skin burns where she's just touched me. "Traffic at this time of day is horrendous."

There are no thoughts in my head. Shock has taken over me. All I can do is gape at her like a goldfish.

She lifts her eyebrows slightly, as if in challenge, and turns to the doctor. "And sorry to you, Doctor. Danielle tends to get nervous at these appointments, so she asked me to tag along."

The lie is so smooth on her lips, it makes me question if I actually *do* get anxious during my appointments.

Doctor Sullivan scrutinizes me for a moment. "Would you like your...friend in here with you, Danielle?"

"Partner," Blair corrects, giving her a wide smile that shows off her pearly whites. "And, of course, it's up to you, sweetheart." Her face has shifted to show concern: eyebrows bunched, eyes wide, a hint of a frown.

This is a mask, I realize. She doesn't feel concern at all—in fact, she may never feel it in any circumstances. But she's able to fool everyone around her.

Everyone except me.

Her expression shifts slightly, as if she can read my thoughts. It's enough to make me steel my spine and smile at my gynecologist. This is a game—and I don't want to lose.

"It's totally fine." I lay myself back and place my feet in the stirrups, refusing to let her get the better of me.

"Slide down," my doctor instructs, which I do, making sure the paper cover doesn't expose me to Blair. I don't think I can handle that.

Blair stands by my head, her fingers gently stroking the side of my neck in a way that the doctor may interpret as comfort, but I know it's a sign of possession. Doctor Sullivan is telling me everything before she does it, and I feel the speculum enter me, but all I can focus on are those damn fingers.

Blair is chatting with the doctor, her face politely animated—she's acting like she's engaged but not to the point that it seems forced. She's good at this, pretending to be a normal person. Has she been doing this her whole life? Who taught her how to mimic others so effectively?

I feel the cotton swab move against my cervix, and I wince. Blair's stormy eyes hold mine, her hand moving to stroke my hair.

"It's all right, Danielle. You're doing so well."

The praise sends shivers down my spine. Oh God, that's why she's here, isn't she? It isn't just about asserting her dominance; it's about making me squirm.

This bitch has a humiliation kink.

A growl builds in my throat, but I shove it down, which earns me her fingers gliding down my throat. I feel myself tighten around the cold metal in me.

Fuck, I'm getting turned on by this. How dare she try to get me excited while my gynecologist has a speculum inside me? I'll never be able to get a pap smear again, too worried about being Pavlov'ed into enjoying it.

Her eyes alight with mischief as Doctor Sullivan eases the tool out of me and says, "All right, go ahead and sit up. I'll call you with the results in a few days. Any questions?"

I shuffle into a seated position, my bare feet leaving the stirrups and dangling in the air. "Nope." I force a smile on my face. "Thanks."

She nods to me before giving Blair a warm smile. "Hope they catch whoever is killing those poor men," she says before standing from her stool and exiting the room.

Leaving Blair and me alone.

"What the fuck?" I whisper-scream, curling my body around itself to hide it from view, to keep some shred of dignity.

Before I can react, Blair snatches my face, hauling me closer until we're nose-to-nose. "And here I was," she breathes, "thinking you were enjoying our little game."

The mask has fallen. It's all her now.

"You have no right to come to my gyno appointment," I snarl in her face.

"I can do whatever I want," she replies matter-of-factly. "Including making you horny like a bitch in heat with that contraption inside of you. Shall we go home and play doctor? I doubt they'll notice a speculum missing here."

Jesus Christ. My pulse jumps at her filthy words, but I need to pull myself together. "We aren't going anywhere together. I am going to leave and go to *my* home, and you're going to go back to hell."

"Now, now, sweetheart, don't be like that. Let me take you out to make it up to you."

I blink in surprise. "Did you not just hear me? I don't want you. I don't want to go *anywhere* with you."

"Yes, you do." She smirks. "Admit it. You put up a convincing fight, but I know the truth. I know you better than you know yourself."

My body is acting of its own accord—my stomach warms at her words, her dominating tone.

Ugh.

"You're insane," I gasp, trying to keep my walls up. I can't let her know she's getting to me.

Her eyes travel over my face, snagging on my mouth. "You wound me." Her words come out in a whisper that caresses my lips.

My breath catches in my throat. What is wrong with me?

Before I can answer my own question, she releases me and steps back. "Get dressed," she commands. "We have a date to start."

Blair has taken me to an ice cream shop.

If I wasn't in shock before, I certainly am now.

We left the doctor's office without incident, except when she grabbed my hand and interlocked our fingers. I snatched my hand away the moment we left the office but kept pace with her as she guided me to the little storefront down the street.

I seriously need to get my head examined. I'm letting this deranged woman stalk me, break into my house, show up at my doctor's appointments, and then take me out for ice cream after.

Blair opens the door to George's Ice Cream, ushering me in. I step in and walk towards the ice cream display. I *do* deserve a treat after that appointment.

I feel her at my back as I smile at the worker behind the counter. "Can I get a small cup of strawberry, please?"

Blair hums thoughtfully as she orders a small cup of coffee ice cream.

I don't even act like I'm going to pay for this; I take my ice cream from the worker and wander to an empty booth as Blair hands over her credit card. She quickly joins me, sliding into the seat opposite me.

"What do you want?" I ask, splaying my hands on the table.

She blinks at me before slowly placing her cup down between us. "Right now, or generally?"

I let out an annoyed huff. "What do you want *with me*?"

Blair tilts her head, her gray eyes roving over my face. "You're angry," she guesses.

"I'm..." Yes, I'm angry, but I'm also confused. And a little horny. "I just want to know why you're doing this to me. You break into my house, but order a fancy security system and send me gifts. You tell me that I'm like you, but provide no further explanation. What kind of game is this?"

"It isn't a game," she says simply, as if that makes it any better.

Her evasiveness sets my teeth on edge. I lean forward and lower my voice. "Just tell me what your deal is. Why are you doing this to me?" *Why are you making me feel so untethered?*

She rolls her shoulders before speaking. "I sensed something in you. I think you're like me."

Her words make my head spin. "You think I'm like you? I've never stalked anyone before and have no desire to."

Blair's eyes narrow. "I can sense a darkness within you that needs nurturing."

I snort. "A darkness, huh? Stop bullshitting me."

"I'm not. I believe you are bogged down by society's expectations of women. You force yourself to act like others, but that isn't who you truly are." She leans back in her seat. "We are alike in that way—except you think that is the only way to be, whereas I know it isn't but choose to behave appropriately."

"The way you behave is not appropriate," I scoff.

"I've never done this to a normal person," she argues. Her saying 'normal' makes me furrow my brows. "I know how they'd react, and I have no interest in going to jail. Besides, they're beneath me and provide me with no stimulation. Unlike you."

I shake my head, unease and disbelief flooding my system. "What *are* you?" I'm afraid to hear the answer, but I have to know.

She shrugs. "*We* are similar, Danielle. You just don't know it yet." She lifts her spoon to her mouth, licking it clean before swallowing and putting it back in the cup. "I don't feel things the way others do. Most emotions are foreign to me. I see others experience them, but I never feel them myself. I feel certain emotions, like anger, but my emotions do not guide my decisions. Most of the time, I don't feel much of anything. I'm bored. Numb."

She licks her lips as her eerie eyes hold mine. "Until I met you. You've made me feel alive."

Heat rushes to my face and my stomach flips—but not in fear, like it should. I try to shove it down. I can't admit I felt the tug between us, like a thread is keeping us tied together. She's clearly unwell and confirming that I felt it too will only embolden her behavior.

She continues, "I've watched you to see if I was right. You have anger issues; you think you're better and smarter than everyone around you, and that makes you feel alone."

I fight with the surprise that bubbles under my skin. "I don't have anger issues."

She rolls her eyes. "Yes, Danielle, you do. You're easily agitated."

Aggravation flares in me, basically confirming her point. I don't like this–it feels like she's stripped me bare and can see every ugly, unsavory part of me.

I need to get away from her. I force the words out. "I need you to leave me alone."

She blinks, her only show of surprise before her face becomes neutral. "No. I can't do that."

"You have to," I argue. "This isn't right—"

"That doesn't matter," she growls, her nostrils flaring. "Forget what you think is right and wrong. We live by our own rules, our own set of morals. Aren't you tired of suffering under the weight of the world's expectations?"

Yes, the voice in the back of my head whispers. *Yes, yes.*

She keeps going. "You're scared. You're scared of what it will mean if you let yourself be the person you're supposed to, but you don't need to be. I will help you."

"Yeah, help me all the way into a psychiatric facility," I mutter. "Look, I'm not sure what you think you felt, but it stops here."

"You need me." She leans forward and grips my wrist, her fingers clamping down. A spark of electricity travels up my arm at the touch.

"Like hell I do," I snap. "Let go of me."

"Never."

She yanks on my arm, pulling me forward until I'm nearly laying across the table. My eyes dart around to see if anyone is witnessing this, but it's November, so no one else has come in for ice cream, and the guy working here has gone to the back.

"I'll make sure you're protected and grounded while you work through this, while you take your mask off for the first time. We'll work through it together."

I'm seething now. I try pulling myself from her grasp. "I don't need shit from you."

"No? Not even help with a certain ex?"

I still. "What?"

"I know he still calls. He threatens you, says horrible things to you. Why?"

"Ask him yourself," I seethe.

She releases me, and I hit the back of my seat. "He should never be allowed to speak again after what he's said to you."

"I agree," I reply before I can stop myself. It feels good to be honest.

Blair seems to sense it, because her mouth lifts slightly, even though her eyes still hold her anger. "I can take care of him."

My eyebrows furrow. "How?"

"You know how."

My eyes widen, finally understanding her meaning. "You mean, kill him?" I force my face to express disgust. She can't be serious—she might be unhinged, but she's not actually a killer. "He doesn't know where I am, and he won't figure it out. Really, he isn't a problem."

She purses her lips, clearly not liking my answer, but she doesn't push it. Instead, she reaches for me again. To my shock, I let her. Her fingers graze the inside of my wrist, igniting the nerve endings in my entire arm. I suck in a breath, trying to stop my pulse from jumping. Her stormy eyes study my face, and it feels like time is standing still.

The moment is broken by the sound of the guy behind the counter sweeping the floor. I turn my head and look out the window, needing a moment to think—and I can't think with her staring me down.

I know I need to leave, to make it clear we are never seeing each other again. But the words don't come.

What is wrong with me? Am I destined to let horrible people into my life so they can fuck it up however they see fit?

I'm lost in my thoughts until Blair clears her throat, demanding my attention. I can't look at her, so I close my eyes. "What?"

"It's clear you need time to think about what I've said." I don't deign to respond. It doesn't dissuade her, though. "I will give you some space, but not for long, so you should hurry up and pull yourself together."

My eyes fly open and I throw her a nasty look. "How generous of you."

She smirks, which sets me off. I pull myself out of the booth, leaving my melted ice cream cup for her to discard.

"I'll give you a week," she calls at my retreating back.

I leave the ice cream shop, stomping to my car in the parking lot across the street. My aggravation keeps building in me as I drive home.

A week. She thinks she can decide how long I can have to get over something? I don't think so.

Clearly it won't be enough to ignore her or to tell her to leave me alone.

I need to beat her at her own game.

I just have no idea how to do that. But I'm determined to figure it out.

Chapter 22

Blair

Danielle seems to be struggling to find sleep tonight.

I watch her from the camera feed as she tosses and turns, her brows pinched together as she flips onto her other side.

What is she dreaming of?

I stop doodling her in my sketchbook and lift my fingers to stroke her face on the screen. I want to go there, to watch over her, to even lay next to her. It feels like there's a string connecting us, and it tugs at me every time I'm away from her, desperate to be near again.

But I told her that she has a week to figure out her feelings.

I shouldn't have offered that. What an incredibly foolish thing to do. It's only been thirty-six hours, and I feel like I'm dying.

I can't wait any longer.

Chapter 23
Danielle

The tombstones bring me a sense of peace.

Maybe because death is the only thing we have in common with one another. Maybe because it's the only thing that is both known and unknown to us.

Or it could be because a cemetery is where my father's bones remain, keeping him from hurting anyone ever again.

Sighing, I lean my head against the stone, letting the crisp, early morning air wake me up. I've always been drawn to cemeteries, to their beauty, their gentle nature. I found this one by accident one afternoon, drawn to it somehow. Its massive grounds look to be well taken care of, but I rarely see anyone here.

Which is perfect for me.

I take a few breaths, forcing myself to not think about Blair and what a strange predicament I've found myself in with her. I hate how she affects me, how easily she gets under my skin.

How I feel like I'm allowing her to stalk me.

I close my eyes, trying to force these thoughts from my head. Only Blair is responsible for her actions. Her stalking me, ultimately, has nothing to do with me. I need to get that through my thick skull before I do something stupid.

I keep focus on my breathing, trying to get rid of my annoyance, when I feel...something. A presence of some sort.

I'm not a believer in ghosts, but I can sense something near.

I open my eyes and see a person in the distance. Squinting, I try to see what direction they're going—it'll be too awkward if I'm just hanging out at their loved one's grave.

Whoever they are, they seem to be walking towards me. I get up, wiping my butt for any leaves or dirt and wander down another path to avoid them.

As soon as I change course, they do too.

I pause and try to see them better. They seem to be dressed in all black, with a hood over their face, so I can't make out any features.

Something in me says to keep walking, so I head in another direction, hoping this is just my mind playing tricks on me. I follow the path, keeping my ears perked and my eye peeking for this person.

They're still coming towards me. I walk a bit faster, anxiety climbing up my throat. Are they going to yell at me for being here? That would be ridiculous, and none of their business.

It isn't until the person gets close enough for me to see that they've removed their hood, revealing a Ghostface mask staring back at me.

"Oh fuck," I breathe.

Blair has come for me.

I don't stop to think before I break into a sprint, trying to put as much distance between us. I don't look back to see if she's running, too—I just keep going, my arms pumping, breath sawing in and out of my lungs. My car is in the opposite direction. I need to turn around so I can get the fuck out of here.

Hooking a left, I dart behind a mausoleum, pressing my back into the stone as I fight to catch my breath. What the fuck is she doing? She's getting bold, showing up wherever I am. She's escalating. Soon, she'll lock me in my house and never let me out.

I need to get to my car. Then drive it to Canada or something. Then get a flight to Antarctica. Somewhere she'll never follow me.

"Okay, I can do this," I murmur. I peel myself off the wall and peek around the corner. No sign of anyone. Just a quiet, empty cemetery. I take a few cautious steps around the side of the mausoleum, ready to make a run for it, just in case, when strong arms wrap around me from behind.

I'm pinned to a chest as arms restrict my own, making escape impossible.

A shriek erupts from my lungs, panic overriding my system. I'm being fucking kidnapped, she's going to kill me—

A gloved hand covers my mouth and I thrash, trying to break free. The smell of leather fills my nostrils. "Hush, Danielle. You'll wake the dead."

Blair's sultry voice fills my ears, making me thrash even harder. "Get the fuck off!" I scream into her hand, but it comes out muffled.

She lifts me off the ground and backs us behind the mausoleum. I kick my feet, trying to dislodge her, but it's no use; her arms are wrapped around me like a vice.

"I've missed you," she croons in my ear. "I'm sure you've missed me too."

"Fuck off," I snarl into the glove.

She *tsk*s and places my feet back on the ground. "I thought we were finally getting somewhere." Her arms tighten around me. "If I remove my hand, you'll have to promise not to scream. Understand?"

I nod furiously.

Blair releases my mouth, and immediately, I shout, "Help! Somebody he—"

Before I can make sense of what's happening, I'm being spun around and pinned against the cool stone. Her haunting eyes meet mine, her mask seemingly discarded among the tombstones.

"Naughty brat," Blair growls before her mouth lands on mine.

I'm too stunned to do anything. My body completely freezes as her lips move against my own in a demanding fashion. My brain has officially gone offline.

Sparks light up my body from within, originating from my mouth, where we're connected. Suddenly, I'm kissing her back urgently, ferociously. I don't even know who I am anymore—I've been taken over by my hormones.

Blair kisses me back with fervor, as if this is her lifeline. Her gloved hands tug at my jacket, exposing my shoulders and breasts to the chilling air. I whimper against her mouth, desire freely flowing through me. My hands reach up and tangle in her hair, the silky strands running through my fingers as Blair breaks the kiss. She plants kisses down my neck, stopping at my collarbones for a moment, before dipping to my exposed nipples. The warmth of her mouth around one makes my eyes roll back in my head.

"Oh," I whisper as pleasure keeps building in me.

Her tongue flits against me, and I groan. The warring sensations of hot and cold wrap around me, making my vision blur.

Blair moves to my other nipple, leaving the first to fend for itself in the cold. The chill feels stronger now than it did before. I press her head to me, as if to keep her there, to warm my body with her mouth.

But it's Blair we're talking about, and she does what she wants. She pops off my breast and straightens, her stormy eyes holding mine. "I bet you're soaked."

I want to fight back, to tell her that isn't true, but we both know that would be a lie. She gives me a smirk as a gloved hand snakes under my waistband. The cool fabric of her glove against me makes me gasp.

Her fingers explore me, spreading me open, caressing my clit, before pulling back out. She raises her hand to show me and snickers.

"Dripping," she purrs before placing them on my lips. "Open."

For some fucking reason, I listen. Her fingers enter my mouth, and I suck on them instinctively, tasting myself on her glove. Blair gently pumps her fingers in and out of my mouth, making sure I get my fill.

It turns me on even more.

I moan against her fingers just as she pulls them out. A triumphant look crosses her face as she steps back. "It's a bit cold to be out here half-naked, isn't it?"

And just like that, the heat from this encounter leaves me. I grab at my clothes, trying to cover myself. "Fuck you," I snarl. "You're supposed to be leaving me the hell alone."

The smirk only widens. "According to your body, that isn't what you want." She lifts her hood and saunters away from me.

All I'm able to do is shout, "Asshole!" at her retreating back, reeling from what the hell just happened.

I watch her as I try to catch my breath. If this sick game wasn't out of control before, it certainly is now. She won't keep her distance; if anything, she's become emboldened. The problem is, I don't know how to play this game with her. There are no rules, no cheat codes. It's a game she created and decides how to play, all on her own.

I march back to my car, spurred on by my irritation. I can figure this out, I know I can. I'm not going to simply lie down and let her win.

No, I'm going to create my own rules.

Chapter 24
Blair

I can't resist her.

Having her lean into me, kiss me back, demanding more, was all I needed. She wants me just as much as I want her.

Finally, we can stop pretending. I'm growing tired of this push-and-pull we're doing. It's time for her to realize what a great team we would be. That we belong together.

Now, easing my way through her front door, I can't help but feel warmth spread through my bones.

She can deny that she's like me, but she won't be able to resist the energy between us. I watched her struggle and fail to do it today, which means even more time together is the only solution.

I float up the stairs and to her bedroom, my heart pounding as I push back her door.

To find her bed empty.

I blink and pull my phone from my pocket, checking the footage again. The screen shows me Danielle, asleep on her bed. I rewind the footage, confused, until I notice that the footage has been looped.

I'd be pissed if I wasn't so impressed. She took my tools and used them herself. Clever girl.

I put my phone away and turn to check the other rooms, confident she's somewhere else in the house, when I spot a laptop in the middle of the bed, right next to her cell phone.

She must think I put a tracker in her phone, which isn't true. At least, not yet.

Going over to the bed, I ease open the laptop to find a video open on the home screen. I hit the spacebar, and Danielle's face comes into view.

She's sitting on the edge of the bed in a black lace bra and panties, her voluptuous body on full display for the camera.

"Hi Blair," she croons at the camera—at me. "If you're watching this, you're probably wondering where I am." She trails a finger down her neck and between her breasts. "I knew you wouldn't be able to stop, so I decided to play the game, too. If you can find me before the sun comes up, you can have me." Her fingers continue their descent down her body, past her navel. "I haven't left any clues, but I know you can do it." Her hand has reached her panties now. "If you don't find me in time, whatever twisted, fucked up thing we have is over. Good luck." Just as her fingers dip inside her waistband, the video cuts off.

My skin feels hot, and my heart is hammering in my chest. I slam the laptop down with more force than necessary.

I pace around the room, my agitation growing with every step. Frankly, I'm offended. She thinks she can outsmart *me*? She can't even accept herself for who she is. If she had thought about this more carefully, she would have asked herself if I was tracking her car.

I can't place blame solely on her, though, as I've clearly been sloppy. Looks like I'll have to put a tracker inside her body.

A sense of...worry comes over me, marrying with my annoyance. Maybe she's not as similar to me as I thought. After all, I wouldn't have foolishly run off and left someone a tantalizing video.

I shake my head, trying to pull myself together. No, my instincts are never wrong. She's just entrenched in how she's been told to be, how she believes she should act. Once she lets the mask fall, she'll be ready for anything.

Pulling my phone out again, I open it up to her car's location.

Looks like she's at a hotel a few towns over.

Part of me wants to *not* go to her, just to see what she'll do next. She obviously doesn't want things to end between us—she'll find a way to see me.

But the other, more animalistic part of me can't resist her. To have her writhing underneath me, whimpering my name as I bring her to the edge, over and over.

A serpentine grin slithers across my face. Let the games begin.

Chapter 25
Danielle

Sitting on the king-sized bed in my hotel room, I peruse the TV channels absentmindedly. Blair won't be able to find me here, an hour away from town. Even if she narrows down my general location, which she has no way of doing, she'd have to visit at least ten different hotels.

The voice in the back of my head keeps reminding me that she's managed to find me before—at the store, my doctor's appointment, the cemetery. It made me wonder if she's done something to my phone. Which is why it's switched off and at home.

It's also why I booked this hotel on my laptop, just in case. Hopefully, this cuts Blair off from me.

I settle against the pillows when I hear a knock on the door. That must be the food I ordered.

"Coming!" I tell them, pulling myself from the pillow fort I've made and rushing to the door. I ease it open and pop my head out, only to find that it isn't my food delivery.

It's Blair.

A little squeak passes my lips and I duck back into the room, throwing my weight into shutting the door just as her hand curls around the frame. She thwarts my efforts easily, the force making me stumble backwards as she breezes in.

"Well, well, well," she purrs. All the blood rushes from my face as I back into the bed at a strange angle, causing me to fall backwards onto the mattress. I scurry to get away, but she lunges, grabbing my ankle and tugging me back to her. "I have to say, I'm disappointed. A chain hotel?" She *tsks*. "I thought you had class."

"How did you find me so quickly?" I squawk.

"If you have to ask, you'll never know."

I bare my teeth at her, aggravation reaching forward.

She continues, "You underestimate us both. Once you shed this false version of yourself, you'll be unstoppable. But now, I get to have you."

Humiliation washes over me. I'm an idiot. I can't believe I thought I could outsmart her. She probably put a tracker under my skin at some point.

I'm too embarrassed to argue. I *did* leave her a scandalous video and told her the rules: if she found me, she could have me. I just didn't expect to be such shit at this game.

And if I'm being truly, brutally honest with myself...I wanted her to find me.

Blair pulls me to the edge of the bed and positions herself in between my legs, looming over me. "Shirt off."

I lock eyes with her and see nothing but pure hunger in them. It's enough to knock me from my embarrassment and quickly discard my sleep shirt, not even caring that I'm not wearing a bra. That electric pulse between us revs up, warming my skin. The hairs on my arms stand on end. Her look is like a brand as she moves down my bare chest.

"Perfect," she murmurs, her voice rough. Her gloved fingers graze across my cheek, slowly moving down my throat until she caresses my clavicle. That energy, the electrical current, runs between us. Sparks dance in my veins, waking every nerve ending, heightening every one of my senses.

Blair cocks her head, as if sensing the shift. "Turn around," she demands. "On all fours."

A gasp passes my lips as arousal ignites in my stomach. A tiny voice, most likely the only sane part of me, tells me this is a terrible idea. She's dangerous. She could hurt me. Even kill me.

Still, I find myself flipping over and getting on my hands and knees, just as instructed. I grip the sheets in my fists as the bed dips with her weight. I want to turn around, to look at her, to know what she wants—

Her hands gently pull my pajama shorts down, exposing me to her. My cheeks flame. Even though I knew this would happen, it's still unnerving to be exposed while she isn't.

I hear her suck in a breath as her hands skate over my ass, caressing my skin. The leather feels cool to the touch, and I shiver.

"Don't move," she instructs, one hand traveling closer and closer to where I need it.

"What if I don't want this?" I manage to squeak out.

Her hand doesn't pause its descent. "Do you not?"

"I—" *I do,* my body shouts at me. But this isn't about my body; it's about my dignity. How will I be able to face her—face anyone—after letting her break into my home and fuck me?

My feelings battle for dominance inside of me.

"You'll need a safe word," she prompts. "If you want it to stop, simply say that word, and I will stop."

"Will you stop breaking into my house and watching me sleep?"

"Is that what you want?"

Yes. No. Oh God, what's wrong with me?

"I don't know," I finally answer, because it's the truth.

Part of me is horrified she does this, but another...another part wants it so badly.

A hard slap lands on my ass, bringing me back from my spiraling. I yelp and twist to yell at her, but she places a hand on my back and pushes me down, my ass now up in the air while the top half of my body is pressed against the mattress.

"What's the word?" she growls, clearly tired of waiting for me to pull myself together.

"Red," I blurt out. "Red."

"Very good."

The praise makes my body tighten with need. Her hand finds itself between my legs, the tip of the leather softly caressing my clit. My toes curl and a small moan passes my lips before I can stop it.

"Greedy," she comments, her finger running back and forth, collecting my arousal. "Hold still," she reminds me as she plunges her finger into me.

A sharp gasp builds in my lungs at the sudden intrusion, at the feel of the leather inside me. She moves in and out slowly, as if she relishes teasing me.

My hips push back to get her deeper. *More,* my body demands. *More, more, more—*

Suddenly, another slap lands, making me jump. "What did I tell you? Don't fucking move."

"Okay, okay, yes," I pant. "I'm sorry—"

Another spank, but this time, her finger inside of me thrusts in and out, setting the punishing pace I need. Another spank, another, another, but I don't even feel them. All I can feel is the leather hitting every nerve inside me.

I moan, letting the pleasure build and build, taking me above my body. She curls her finger just right, making stars dance in my vision as her other hand dips to circle my clit.

"Fuck!" I cry out, the feeling too much, too overwhelming.

"Don't come."

Her words barely register through the pleasure. "What?" I breathe, turning my head so she can hear me. "I can't stop," I whine.

"You can." She says it with such certainty, as if she isn't hitting each spot with perfection. "You don't come unless I say so."

I groan, both from the sensation of her talented, gloved fingers and from her demand. I'll combust if I hold it back.

I don't think I'll survive it.

"Do you understand?" Her finger slows.

"Fuck, yes, I get it!" I snarl, canting my hips. I don't want to lose this orgasm or this game. "I get it, okay, just keep going."

She lets out a huff that I think is a laugh before another finger enters me and she goes back to the brutal pace. "You're soaking me," she comments, sounding awed.

I fold my arms underneath me and press my face into the mattress, biting down on the sheets, willing myself not to come, even though it's the only thing I've ever wanted. I won't give in; I won't let her win.

I filter through my thoughts, trying to think of un-sexy things—anything to stop my orgasm from taking over.

"If you'd like to come, you can beg," she offers.

I feel myself clamp down on her fingers.

Before I can even consider how embarrassing that would be, the words bubble up and out. "Please," I start. "Please let me come."

"You can do better than that."

I groan as another wave of arousal spreads through me. "Can I please come? Please, I need it. I'll do anything for it."

"Anything?" Her voice sounds strained.

"Yes, yes, anything." I don't even know what I'm saying or what I'm agreeing to, but it doesn't matter.

"You'll let me do whatever filthy, dirty thing I want to you?"

I groan. "Yes."

The thrusts become harder. "What if I want to put a collar and leash on you? Will you let me drag you around?"

Christ.

"What about making you drink from a dog bowl while I fuck your ass? Or make you crawl around on all fours with a vibrator shoved inside you?"

The thought of her doing any of those things to me brings tears to my eyes from holding my release back. The noises coming from me aren't even words—they're just pitiful whimpers.

Blair chuckles. "Go ahead, Danielle. Come on my hand."

I don't need to be told twice. My entire body tightens as my orgasm overtakes me, sweeping me away. Cries spill from my lips as pleasure grips me tight, as Blair's fingers expertly glide both in and against me.

When I come back to myself, she eases herself from me, causing little sparks to radiate through me. I feel her weight leave the bed and I pivot, sitting up to face her. I try to regulate my heavy breathing, to lower my heart rate, as if that will bring my dignity back and prove I wasn't as affected by her as I actually was.

It feels like we're in our own world.

She gives me an evil grin and says, "Don't think we're even close to being done, Danielle. I get to have you all night."

I wake up to an empty hotel room.

I'm not surprised. Blair doesn't seem like a 'snuggle and drink coffee in bed' kind of person.

The humiliation at my pathetic attempt to play her game is gone. I wanted her to find me. What she told me at the ice cream shop ping-pongs in my head.

We are similar, Danielle. You just don't know it yet.

She said she doesn't feel many emotions, but I struggle to believe that. I've seen her emotions written on her face—they're subdued, but they're there. A little quirk of her lips, a raised eyebrow...

I get out of bed and head to the bathroom, splashing water on my face as my thoughts keep churning. What if these little tells aren't tells at all? What if it's just another mask she puts on to make me think she's feeling something she isn't?

I shut the water off and press my palms into the counter, not even bothering to dry my face as I take deep, grounding breaths. That must be what it is—she's just letting me see what I want to see.

But...I've seen her mask while it's on, and this feels different. I don't know why, but I sense the true Blair only shows herself to me.

A tiny, incredulous laugh slips past my lips at my naivety. Pushing back from the counter, I dry my face and brush my teeth before going back into the bedroom for my discarded clothes. Quickly getting dressed and pulling myself together, I leave the hotel room I begrudgingly realize I didn't need to pay for—Blair could've come over last night and it would have been the same outcome.

Still, it felt extra hot to do it in a hotel room. It felt almost anonymous, like we could step outside of ourselves for the night. No anxieties, no responsibilities. I could be the sex-hungry slut I wanted to be without reservation.

I lost count of the orgasms Blair pulled from my body. Unfortunately, I didn't get to return the favor. Not that I really could have by the time she was done with me, anyway; I was a sopping, boneless mess.

But it can't happen again, I decide as I hurry to my car. I need answers from her, to help me understand what she's so confident about, and that's it. No more of this.

Blair is sitting on my kitchen island, helping herself to my coffee. I shouldn't be surprised to see her. Wordlessly, I fix myself a cup and take a few sips before setting it down and locking eyes with her.

"I want to know everything there is to know about you. And what, exactly, makes us alike."

Her gray eyes search my face before she replies, "What would you like to know?"

"How did you find me? I didn't leave any hints, yet you found me almost immediately."

Blair scrutinizes me for a moment before answering. "I placed a tracker on your car."

"So, you *are* actually tracking me." I assumed it was possible, but the reality of the situation crashes down on me.

"Just your car. I hadn't gotten around to tracking your phone yet."

A very dangerous person is stalking me. Who knows what she'll do? She could be infatuated with me one moment, then ready to murder me the next.

She can't know where I go, what I'm up to.

For some reason, none of the expected emotions flood my system. I should be freaking out, calling the authorities, or even packing up and moving again.

She's just like Jeremy, I try to tell myself, but it doesn't trigger any alarms in my head.

"Danielle?"

She's broken me somehow; or maybe I was already broken to begin with. That is more dangerous than anything. I need her to leave so I can figure this out.

I square my shoulders and say with as much vitriol as I can, just to convince her that I feel a way I don't. "All of this—the cameras, the tracker on my car—are all avenues to control me."

"No, it isn't. I have no desire to control you."

I shake my head, forcing myself to show disgust, even though it's fake. "This behavior is just the beginning. Next, you'll think it's okay to put your hands on me."

Her stormy eyes widen slightly in shock. "Danielle, I would never do that to you."

I let out a humorless laugh. "That's what they all say."

"Who?" she asks, anger splashing across her features. "Did *he* do that to you?"

Forcing tears to my eyes, I whisper, "You have no right to do this."

For once, the confident, assured woman before me seems to be at a loss for words. My acting seems to be working, to my surprise.

"I have no interest in controlling or harming you. I mean it. I simply wanted..." She releases a harsh breath. "I see a darkness in you that looks like mine. Yours is deeper, hidden behind society's expectations, but it's there, growing larger every moment. I wanted to help that darkness come forward."

"I don't know what that means," I nearly shout, my frustration sizzling.

She sighs and hops down from the counter, moving so that the island is between us. "I've never been like other people. I don't feel things the way everyone else does."

She pulls out the bar stool and sits, leaning her forearms against the marble and staring at me, through me, in that unflinching way of hers. "I didn't understand it when I was growing up. Why did the other kids cry at the drop of a hat?" She shakes her head. "It didn't make sense to me. It wasn't until I got a bit older that I realized *why* I was different."

"You don't feel anything," I guess.

"I don't feel much," she corrects me. "I'm not driven by my emotions; they don't cloud my judgment."

I snort. "Really? You've never made a decision based on your feelings?" It sounds like an impossible thing for a human, to experience life without emotions.

"I haven't."

"Then what do you call this?" I gesture to us. "What do you consider stalking me?"

"Research. Assistance."

I roll my eyes. "Cut the bullshit."

Her eyebrows narrow slightly. "I'm not lying. I sensed that you were like me, so I followed that instinct. While I may not have empathy, I *do* have issues with impulsiveness."

An incredulous laugh rises in my throat. "You want me to believe that you have no empathy, and that I also don't have any, and that's why you're terrorizing me."

"I'm not terrorizing you." She rolls her eyes. "Admit it, you enjoy what we're doing."

I ignore that. "I don't believe you."

"Why not?"

"Because aren't people like you..." Serial killers or locked away somewhere? I switch gears. "I have feelings. I cry at sad movies, and I get angry when people are being stupid or drive badly—"

She cuts me off. "I didn't say you don't have feelings. It's fine if you have them." It sounds very much like it is *not* fine, like it's actually an inconvenience. "What I'm saying is that you let your emotions run amok and they control you, when you have the power to control them. Humans are just animals, driven by impulse. But at least animals aren't blinded by emotions. People react with such disregard to logic, simply because of their *feelings*." She says the last word like those are completely beneath her.

Her words make my stomach clench. I've always had trouble controlling my feelings, specifically anger. It always seems to be simmering just under the surface, waiting for a minuscule temperature change to send it into a boil.

But whatever. Everyone lets their emotions get away from them every once in a while. I figured that was normal.

Well, normal for everyone besides Blair, apparently.

"What happens when you see something sad, or scary, or something happens that makes you mad?"

She shrugs. "I see things that would be considered sad, but I don't know the feeling. I've seen people act like they're upset—their faces contorted, tears pooling, snot dribbling." She scrunches her nose as if she's disgusted. "I've never felt anything that would make me react that way. Fear seems to make me feel excited, instead. It's a rush of adrenaline that I find enjoyable. And as for anger…" She chuckles. "Anger is one emotion I know very well. People like us are tapped into that feeling."

"Don't say us," I snap.

She gives me a feral grin.

"But do you ever feel anxious?"

"No," she replies. "I've never felt anxious about anything."

I snort. "Must be nice."

She shrugs, clearly nonplussed. "You're anxious because you care about what others think. But why bother? They're beneath you."

I reach for my coffee and take a sip before responding, "I can't just…go around and act like I'm better than everyone."

"Why not?" she pushes. "You are."

I know, I nearly say, catching myself off-guard. I mean, I have jokingly said I'm always surrounded by morons, but I don't actually believe that. It's just when someone fucks up a simple task at work, or someone is not paying attention while driving, or…

Blair nods. "Exactly," she says as if I said my train of thought out loud. "You already know the truth; it's just about if you will let it guide you."

I shake my head, trying to dislodge this train of thought. "That isn't a productive or sane way to go about life."

The corners of her mouth quirk up. "Why do you think I have so much fun manipulating all of the idiots around me?"

I expect a slimy feeling to come over me at her words, but...it doesn't. "How do you do that?" I ask.

She shrugs. "I like to push their buttons to see how they'll react, to see how they'll lash out at someone. People are so quick to grasp at control, at any sense of dominance." She drinks before continuing. "Sometimes, all I do is sit and listen. People love to talk about themselves—listen long enough, and they'll divulge some truly morally questionable beliefs. They feel safe to share with me because I don't judge them."

"But you *do* judge them," I argue.

"In a way, but not because they think about the things they do. I judge them for not acting on these beliefs."

Blair's words sound...liberating. No anxiety? Sign me up for that. Perhaps recognizing that I'm better than everyone and not expecting them to rise to the occasion will stop me feeling so overwhelmed all the time.

"I'm worried," I blurt out, the truth fighting to come forward.

"About what?"

That I'm not as scared as I should be. "That you'll hurt me. That you'll manipulate me, just like you do with everyone else." The lie falls smoothly from my lips–maybe part of me *is* worried about this.

She scrutinizes me for a moment. "I have no desire to do that to you. Besides, you are more than capable of doing the same to me. Perhaps even more so." I want to press her on that, but she continues. "I have no reason to lie to you."

"You just told me that you like to manipulate people," I point out.

"I was doing that to you, at first—in a way," she clarifies at the horrified expression on my face. "I had to see your reactions to different situations, just to make sure we were alike." She gives me a contented smile. "And we are–although, your rage really takes center stage in your life. But once I knew who you were, I began to fixate on you, on having you. I enjoy who you are, and I can't let you go."

This woman is dangerous. And even worse, I may be just like her. I steel my spine and force myself to do what I had set out to do. I got my answers and now this is done.

"We can't keep doing this."

She tilts her head slightly. "Why not?"

"Because..." It's wrong, so wrong. I shouldn't feel this way about someone who does things like this. "Because you're wrong about me. I'm not who you think I am."

"Stop lying." Her nostrils flare.

"I'm not." It doesn't even sound convincing. "You're no different than any other person who hurts people. I won't let you do that to me."

"I won't."

I shake my head, closing my eyes for a moment. "Just go, Blair."

"No." Her hands are trembling. "You're pushing me away because you think you're afraid. Let go of that."

"Blair." My voice comes out in a rasp. "Please leave."

"You're stuck with me," she growls. "If you try to push me out, I'll come back each time. If you try to leave, I'll follow. Try to run, and I'll hunt you down and drag you back."

My blood is singing at her words. I push past the feeling of...rightness that comes over me and say, "Get out of my house."

Blair blinks. A moment of charged silence flows between us. I half-expect her to reach across the island and grab me, but she doesn't. Instead, she clears her throat and stands.

"Fine."

She strides out of the kitchen without another word. I hear my front door open and close a moment later, letting me know I'm all alone.

Chapter 26

I'm getting really good at this.

"Please," the man groans, his voice barely above a whisper. His blood coats his bare chest. I lost count of how many slashes I've made into his flesh. "Please, I have money—"

I scoff. The voice in my head is quiet tonight, as if it knows I no longer need it. "I'm not doing this for money."

He can't seem to comprehend that. He sputters for a few moments before I say, "I'm doing this because the world will be a better place without you in it."

A whimper passes his lips as he begins to cry. I bring the blade down, one final time.

Chapter 27
Danielle

It's been a week since Blair was in my house.

A week since I told her that whatever we were doing had to end. That she needed to leave me alone.

I'll admit, I'm shocked she actually listened. That first night, I was confident she'd show up in my bedroom. I waited up all night, my body refusing to let me settle enough to fall asleep.

But she didn't show. Same as the next night, and the night after.

No sign of her at work, either.

Each passing day with no sign of her aggravates me. I walk around with a nasty look on my face, daring anyone to come near. I'm shocked HR hasn't called me into their office to discuss my piss-poor attitude.

I know I'm being unreasonable. I should be happy she's fucked off, but for some reason, I'm not. I try to tell myself she's probably moved on to someone else to obsess over, but that just leaves this unhappy pit in my stomach.

Everything has gone wrong today. I slept through my alarm and had to skip a shower before work. I forgot I was low on gas, so I had to stop at a gas station in the opposite direction of work because they're the only one who takes my grocery store gas points. And as I pulled into the parking lot, I lifted my coffee by the lid that I somehow incorrectly screwed on, and it spilled all over my pants.

On top of it all, my mother called me to say Jeremy stopped by to see her. I nearly had smoke shooting out of my ears.

Luckily, the office is quiet. Everyone is in their holiday lull, where they're really just waiting until the new year to do any work.

I find myself pulling up the home security app on my phone as I sit at my shared table. Will she stop by today? A big part of me hopes so. It would be super awkward if I got ghosted by my own stalker.

A smaller, quieter part of me wants her to because...I like it.

It's sick to want her, I know. Stalkers are scary, deranged people who will eventually hurt their victims. But, for some inexplicable reason, I can't stop thinking about her.

I've gone through every scenario and know she's dangerous and that she could hurt me, but my panic around her being like Jeremy doesn't seem to materialize.

Her words about not wanting to hurt me bounce around in my brain.

I'm scared of her, but it's more in a...sexy way?

Humiliation washes over me. *This is ridiculous,* I scold myself. I can't trust my gut instinct on if she's dangerous or not—she's clearly unwell and has no sense of boundaries. Even if she won't hurt me, even if she isn't like Jeremy, I have to stop. I can't encourage this behavior.

I keep the security footage of my house up anyway.

I let out a groan. My thoughts are racing a mile a minute as time creeps past with no sign of her. No packages dropped off. No cutting of the cameras. Nothing.

I slump back in my chair, disappointment snaking through my veins. "Get a grip," I tell myself before angrily closing the app and placing my phone face down. I can't let our time in the hotel cloud my judgment about her, about all of this. This is just some sick game she wanted to play, and now that she's won, the game is over.

Leaning my head against the back of my chair, I daydream what it would be like if *I* started stalking *her*. Would she like that? Would it make her feel scared or on edge? Or would it remind her of why she was so fascinated with me in the first place?

I can't think like this. This woman has managed to worm herself under my skin, making me consider committing a literal crime just because she ghosted me. I shudder, thinking about how men do crazy shit like this all the time.

Shaking my head, I glance at the clock on my computer monitor and notice it's 4:48PM. I stand from my chair and peek around, on the lookout for my one nosy coworker who will tattle if I leave early. Not seeing or hearing her, I shut down my computer, gather my belongings, and silently slip out.

The autumn air is cooler than it was on my lunch break, easing us into winter. Leaves on the concrete flutter around as a gust of wind barrels into me, sending my curls into a tizzy around my face.

As I get into my car and drive home, I begin my plan of releasing myself from Blair's hold. No way is she going to cause my demise.

I mull over what she's told me, what she wants from me. She thinks I have no empathy, no true range of emotions, which is ridiculous. I may prefer others to keep their distance, but that doesn't mean I don't understand people. The problem is that most people are stupid and selfish and will act accordingly. Most of the time, I'm walking around, agitated with everyone. My first instinct isn't to empathize with others.

But I have friends. I've always kept my circle small, but I have them. Sure, I don't feel the need to see them or speak to them all that much, but I love them and would do anything for them.

I wouldn't feel that way if I didn't have feelings, right? Isn't that a basic requirement for relationships?

Her mention of my anger nags at me. I'm angry a lot—constantly on edge, ready to shout at someone or hit someone with my car. I assumed my rage came from being mistreated and abused for so long, but maybe it's always been there. It simmers under the surface, climbing to a boil as my tolerance for dealing with shit erodes.

A frustrated sigh passes my lips as I continue my drive home. It's like Blair has thrown a grenade into my new life and it's about to destroy everything. I've worked tirelessly to build myself back up after everything came crashing down, and I've let this woman waltz in here, hell bent on tearing it apart.

I can't let her do that, but I fear it's too late.

A tiny part of me—well, a large part—doesn't want her to stay away, even if it's just to answer questions I have about myself.

Maybe she'll prove me wrong, and this won't destroy everything.

Or maybe I just want to see what she does with the wreckage.

Pulling into my garage after my commute home, I've made up my mind.

I stomp out of my car, out of the garage, and right up to my front door. Leaning down so I'm eye-level with my new fancy doorbell, I snarl, "Listen here, you motherfucker. You win, okay? I don't know how you managed it, but you've wormed under my skin and now I can't think about anything else." I can't believe I'm shouting at my door. "Are you happy now?"

Straightening, I flip off the doorbell before trudging inside.

Chapter 28
Blair

Each second that's passed since I left Danielle has been agony. It took all my willpower to stay away from her, just like she asked—no, demanded.

It makes me agitated. She doesn't know what's good for her like I do. She's going about this the wrong way. Instead of running away from this, she should be leaning into it, accepting it.

I've avoided looking at the camera feed because I knew seeing her would drag me back under her spell, even going as far as turning off all notifications.

I can't believe I've held out this long. Usually, I just do what I want. But with Danielle, I don't want to bulldoze my way through. Granted, that's what I've been doing since I met her, but I want her to come to her senses on her own.

I want her to want me, and even though I'd like to, I can't force that.

So, I've left her alone. It's made me irritable beyond belief.

"I hate watching the news." My sister shudders as the news anchor on TV reports another potential murder in the area. We're in her kitchen, preparing dinner while her husband plays with the kids in the other room. Ariana is nervously peeling the carrot in her grasp. "I saw online that there's social media influencers who think the murders are all connected."

I feel one of my eyebrows raise slightly. "Oh?"

She nods before pointing at the TV with the carrot peeler. "They claim all the victims know each other." Her eyes get a distant look in them. "Or maybe it was just that they follow each other's accounts. I can't remember now." She shakes her head. "It's scary. Three men in the last two months?"

That's a curious theory. I'll have to ask Cherry, my sole connection to the underground crime world, about it the next time I see her.

"Sounds like a new serial killer," I muse.

Ariana nearly chokes on air, her eyes wide as saucers. "Don't say that," she tells me in a hushed tone. "I can't deal with any stress right now." Sighing, she drops the vegetable and rubs her swollen belly. "My obstetrician told me that my blood pressure is high, and if it doesn't go down by my next appointment, they'll have to induce me."

"That sounds logical," I respond, going back to slicing the cucumbers on the cutting board.

"But I don't want to be induced," she moans, her mouth wobbling and tears forming in her eyes.

I fight the urge to roll my own. This isn't really something to cry about. "You want the baby to be healthy," I point out. "If inducing you is the safest option for both of you, then it makes sense to me."

She bursts into tears, doing exactly the opposite of what I hoped for. "It just won't be the same," she wails. "I wanted an unmedicated birth, like I had with Emma and Jack." She wipes her tears with the back of her hand. "I just want *one thing* to go right."

I'm not really sure what to say to that. Ariana knows how I feel about her deadbeat husband, but she stays with him, anyway. The only reason I don't strangle him to death is because she seems to love him. He doesn't put his hands on her and doesn't treat her unkindly—at least, that I'm aware of—so I let him live.

My sister sniffles. I rein in my exasperated sigh and offer blandly, "I'm sure everything will work out."

Thankfully, that seems to do the trick, because she waves her hands and lets out a small chuckle. "Oh, gosh, I'm sorry. It's just that I'm so hormonal right now, and having two kids already is a lot." She gives me a watery smile. "Thank you for coming over to help me, by the way. It's nice to spend some time together."

"Yep."

She wipes the remnants of her tears and says, "No more talk of depressing things. What's going on in your life? How's work?"

I shrug. "Nothing interesting." I put the knife down and scoop the cucumber into the large bowl awaiting them.

"Are you seeing anyone?"

My mind quickly plays through the pros and cons of telling my sister about Danielle. If I tell her, she'll have a million questions and will probably want to meet her. Would Danielle ever agree to something like that?

I must be quiet for a while because Ariana elbows me gently in the ribs. "You are, aren't you?" She gasps and claps her hands together. "You must tell me everything! What's their name? How did you meet?"

Fuck it. It's not like I'm letting Danielle go, anyway. "Her name is Danielle. We met on Halloween."

Ariana literally squeals. "I've literally never known you to be into someone! I must know every single detail."

I doubt very much that she'll enjoy hearing all of the things I've done to that woman.

She continues, "When can I meet her?"

I shake my head. "Not yet. It's still new." *But it's already a full-blown obsession.*

"Fine, fine, okay. You're right, don't wanna scare her off." She sighs dreamily. "I'm so happy for you, Blair. Really. It's about time you had someone special in your life."

I grunt noncommittally, not really sure of the appropriate response to that.

Luckily, I don't have to, as Emma, Jack, and Ariana's husband burst into the kitchen. "Mom! We're hungry *now*!" my niece whines.

My hand absentmindedly pulls my phone from my pocket, looking to check on Danielle. I consider pushing the urge away, but my resolve has broken. I open the doorbell feed on my phone, a bit surprised to see Danielle speaking at it.

"Blair, come sit," my sister says to me as she gets her kids seated.

"Yeah, one second," I mumble, drifting out of the kitchen to watch the footage of Danielle coming home.

"Listen here, you motherfucker—"

Oh, I'm listening, all right. I listen to her meltdown twelve times, my heart pounding harder with each replay.

She wants me. She *needs* me. She's ready to shed expectations and be who she was meant to be.

I salivate at the thought of seeing her in her true form.

If it was anyone else, I wouldn't care. I would have moved on and not looked back. Other people's lives are not my problem.

But hers...that I care about.

I close my phone and stride back into the kitchen, my irritation evaporating. I'll let Danielle sweat for just a little bit longer, I decide as I take my seat at the table. She's not going anywhere—not when I have her right where she belongs.

Chapter 29

Danielle

If I hated the open concept office before, I hate it even more now.

Everyone is gathered around, mingling with one another as jazz plays from someone's computer.

This office loves to have parties. I've only been here for a few weeks, and so far, we've had six birthdays, a going away party, and a party when the servers went down and we couldn't do any work—although, that was more of an impromptu situation.

Now, it's a Thanksgiving potluck.

I brought my own food, as I do for every single event. My coworkers can never remember my dietary restriction, even though they ask me about it all the time.

Can you eat dairy?

Oh, this has rice in it, so I don't think you can eat it.

What even is gluten?

It's moments like these that make me want to bash someone's head against the wall. I'm sitting off on my own, picking at my salad, lost in my own thoughts. When the office can't accommodate a dietary restriction, it brings out my feral rage, starting me down a spiral of negative thoughts.

Barbara can never convert PDFs. Jason throws his empty plastic water bottles away instead of recycling them. Diane always talks way too loud on the phone.

I can't stand any of them.

To make matters worse, there's still no word from Blair. At this point, I really believe she's going to leave me alone. She probably got bored of the chase and moved onto someone else. I haven't seen her at work, which is upsetting, but at least it's made me productive.

Trying to snap myself out of it, I pull out my phone, bouncing from app to app. There's one in particular that I enjoy perusing—it's a group where people can post shitty men in the area as a warning to others out there. Lately, the posts have surrounded the several disappearances of men in the area. And how all of them were posted on here prior for abusive behavior.

I'm pulled from my phone by the sound of my name, which I nearly miss from the blood pounding in my ears. I look over and see my coworker, Andrew, walking towards me with a plate full of food.

"Mind if I join you?" he asks politely.

I force my face to smile, as I know I've got a nasty look splashed across it. "Of course."

He grins in return before sitting down. The room has a buzz around it as people continue their own conversations. "How come you're not eating the food everyone brought?"

My teeth grind together before I force myself to chill out. "I can't eat any of that."

"Oh." His eyebrows furrow slightly. "Right. Sorry, I forgot. Vegan, right?"

Aggravation is building in me, too quickly for me to quell it. "Nope. I have an autoimmune disorder that will destroy my body if I eat any gluten."

His confusion quickly morphs into unease, making me feel a bit better. Good. I might be acting a bit dramatic, but I want him to be as uncomfortable as I feel.

"Excuse me, I have to go to the restroom," I mutter, rising from my seat and leaving my boring salad and boring coworker behind.

Speed walking to privacy, my agitation is boiling over into anger. My vision goes red as I burst through the bathroom door and rush to a sink, placing my hands upon the cool porcelain.

Pull yourself together. I take a deep breath, then another, then another. I can't flip out over this shit, no matter how much I might want to.

What annoys me is everyone's lack of logic or common sense. Why wouldn't they get food that everyone can eat? Why wouldn't they learn how to convert PDFs, or recycle their plastic, or think about their surroundings for one millisecond?

I'm tired of everyone's lack of awareness, but I can't quit. I need this job. It has good benefits, and the work itself is relatively easy. It's the people that are the problem.

Sighing, I turn the water on and put my hand under the tap. Lifting my wet hand, I place it on the back of my neck and think of what Blair said: *These people aren't worth it. They're beneath you.*

It quickly settles me. She's right about that; they *are* beneath me. I used to feel a twinge of guilt when I thought this, but Blair is making me realize I don't have to. I'm still not sure if it's a good thing.

By the time I pull into my garage, I'm emotionally exhausted. My coworkers asked me, with varying degrees of passive-aggressiveness, why I wanted to leave the party early. I tried to keep my irritation in check, but every time I got asked yet again, I felt like clawing their eyes out.

To make matters worse, traffic was a nightmare. Flurries began bombarding my windshield as I started my commute. I pride myself on being a good driver, after learning to drive in Midwestern winters.

Unfortunately, not everyone here is equipped to drive in inclement weather.

I spent the entire drive screaming obscenities at nearly everyone. My throat is dry, and my nerves are shot as I slam my car door shut and head into the house. I can feel myself becoming overstimulated, like the smallest inconvenience could set me off. I'm a dormant volcano that hasn't erupted in a while.

As I drag myself inside, I kick off my shoes, drop my bag, and rip my coat off me. "I need wine," I grumble to myself, throwing my blouse off as I walk to my kitchen and walk directly to the fridge. I pull the bottle out and take a few drinks straight from it.

"Good evening."

Panic overrides my body as I let out an ear-piercing shriek and pivot to the sound of someone's voice behind me. My hand releases the bottle, and it shatters on the floor next to me, splashing wine all over the place.

Blair sits at my island, in the dark, smirking. She must have seen the entire pathetic image as I guzzled wine in my bra and work pants. The wine that is now soaking my floor.

And I erupt.

"What the *fuck* are you doing in my *house*?!" My scream comes out raspy, but I can't stop. "Who do you think you are?! Get the FUCK OUT!"

She doesn't give me much of a reaction—she just cocks her head, her gray eyes taking in what a sorry state I am. "You should be careful about stepping on the glass."

My mouth hangs open. "Did you not hear me? I said, get. the. fuck. OUT!" Lava is pouring from my ears, leaking from my eyes, dripping down my nose as I rage. "Do you not listen? Do you ever think about anyone but yourself? All you care about is what you want. 'Sure, I'll break into Danielle's house because I want to. Who cares what she wants?' You're a selfish, psychotic asshole."

All filters have been destroyed in the destruction of my anger. I keep screaming at her, telling her how she pushed herself into my life without considering anything but her own wants; how my house belongs to me, not her, and how fucked up it is that she's violating my space; how she's an emotionless robot.

Eventually, the tirade stops. I'm panting, my body feeling worn out, my head pounding. And that's when the realization of what I've said dawns on me.

I swallow nervously. Blair hasn't moved or changed her facial expression. Is she going to snap and hurt me?

"I'm so sorry," I breathe, my throat hurting. "I just...I was—"

Without a word, Blair stands and walks around the island to me. I stiffen, fight or flight trying to kick in, but my brain is incapable of picking one, so I just stand frozen as she gently takes my hands in hers and walks backwards, leading me to walk with her.

"The glass should be cleaned up," she informs me.

The what?

Oh, the wine bottle.

Humiliation and shame heat my body, making me want to hide under a rock. Blair takes me to where she was sitting before dropping my hands and walking to the hall closet. She comes back a few moments later with my broom and dustpan, striding to the mess I made and cleaning it up efficiently. I'm too stunned by the entire turn of events to say anything until Blair is done cleaning the mess.

"I am *so* sorry," I repeat. "I was just having a shit day, and I had just reached my limit, and I wasn't expecting you. I didn't mean what I said."

She prowls over to me, leaning forward so she's towering over me. Her stormy eyes hold mine as I trip over my own tongue to apologize some more.

"You haven't upset me."

I blink in surprise. "I said some really nasty things."

"I'm not offended." She shrugs.

"Really?"

"Really."

"Oh."

She gives me a tiny grin. "Oh." Her face, her stance, make it clear she's telling the truth. "I *did* come into your life because I wanted to. And you're right, I didn't really consider how you would feel." From the way she says it, it's obvious she doesn't feel bad about it. "I want what I want, and I want nothing to stand in my way. I want you, and I will have you."

Her words make goosebumps cover my skin. "I'm scared," I whisper. Scared of the unknown, of what this might unleash in me.

"I know." She gathers me into her arms, her chin resting on the top of my head. To my shock, my own arms wrap around her waist. "I'm here to help you. We'll get through it together."

Her words cause warmth to spread through my body. I realize, in this moment, that I want nothing more.

Chapter 30
Blair

I meant what I told Danielle—I'm not offended or upset by her tirade. She was right, and we both know what I've done to have her. I see no reason to be upset by her saying so.

If she had been anyone else, I would have laughed as she raged, just to rile her up. But I had no interest in doing that; I just wanted her to get it out of her system.

We make our way into the living room and I sit next to her on the couch as she wraps a heavy blanket around her frame.

"I feel like my anger has been out of control," she admits, "even more than usual. I'm not sure if it's from all the change in my life, or from you."

"I haven't made you more angry," I chuckle.

She shoots me a glare. "No, but you fill my head with nonsense."

I scoff. "It isn't nonsense, Danielle. You react this way when others behave in a way that differs from what you think is right. You get angry because you keep seeing these people as your equals." I smooth her curls away from her face. "They are beneath you, Danielle. They will never change; they will never see the world objectively because they are blinded by their emotions. By their code of ethics that bends for different situations, all so they can avoid seeing themselves clearly. I know who you are, even better than you know yourself."

"How?" she asks. "How is that even possible?"

"We have a sense of those that are like us." I shrug. "When I first met you, I knew you weren't what you thought you were."

She gets a distant look in her eye. "I've never really cared for people. I had a very low tolerance for everyone. But I *do* have friends. How can I be like you and have people I care about?"

I roll my eyes. "Contrary to what you've called me, we're not robots. It's entirely possible to have relationships with others—it just may look different. My half-sister and I have a relationship. I would do anything for her, and she loves me, but when I look at her, I don't feel much of anything." I shrug. "She's important to me, but she doesn't conjure up any emotions."

"How do I turn them off?" she asks.

"You focus on the logic instead of the feeling," I instruct. "Recognize the emotion and remove it from the moment."

"Recognize and remove." She nods thoughtfully.

I continue, "Ask yourself why you feel this way and see if the situation warrants that response. Most of the time, it doesn't. The emotions you feel are your masks—just make sure you are aware of when you're wearing them."

She hums. "That makes sense. I always struggled to react appropriately to certain situations." She gives me a crooked smile. "Maybe my emotional wires were getting crossed. I used to think, 'if everyone is feeling this way, then I should too', but it never felt...real."

"Yes," I breathe. "That's exactly right."

Danielle furrows her brows. "But you *do* feel things."

Her statement makes me pause. Haven't we been over this already? "Not many," I reply slowly.

She shakes her head. "No, you do. I see it on your face—"

"My masks are impeccable," I boast.

"*No*," she pushes. "I see them. I see them when you look at me, when you speak to me. You may not experience emotions the same way most people do, but you *do* have feelings. I see them. When you're angry, your shoulders tense, your nostrils flare, and you have a slight frown.

When you're excited, your eyebrows will raise just a hair. When you speak of your sister— someone you love—your eyes soften almost imperceptibly. I have yet to see you sad, but I'm sure you have a tell for that, too."

Her words make me blink.

"And when you're surprised, you blink." She chuckles.

"I—" I'm at a loss for words.

It's true that Danielle has stirred... sensations that are foreign to me. Are those what she's seeing? I've learned to mimic others perfectly through trial and error; the idea that I'm showing an emotion without actively forcing it...

Something in my chest twinges.

"Sounds like we can learn things from one another," she boasts, a smirk spreading across her lips. "You'll teach me how to be more removed, and I'll teach you how to unlock your feelings."

I don't like the sound of that one bit. "And how will you do that?"

"I'm not sure," she admits. "But you seem to feel things with me, so the more time we spend together, the more we'll figure it out."

My heart pounds at the mention of time spent together. "What you've said before, about wanting me to leave you alone, isn't true." It's not a question.

Her tongue darts out to lick her lips nervously. "You scared me at first—not just the stalking, but everything you would tell me. But...I think I'm already heading down this path, anyway."

Yes. Yes, yes, yes—

I reach forward and tangle my fingers in her hair, keeping her locked in place. "You are. And I am going to be here, every step of the way. You're not in charge here, Danielle. I am."

Her eyes alight with annoyance. "You can't tell me what to—"

I press my mouth onto hers, swallowing her arguments, her excuses. *Mine*, my body sings as my lips move with hers.

She doesn't even pretend to put up a fight. A whimper comes from her as she opens for me. My tongue caresses hers and it feels like I'm floating. Danielle cups my face, holding me to her, like she never wants this to end.

Which is good, because I'll never let her go.

My fingers tighten in her hair, pulling gently as we move together. My other hand moves down, urgently ripping the blanket shielding her body.

"You're mine," I growl against her lips. "We're going to be bad together."

"Maybe I'm already bad," she teases breathily.

A smile tugs against my lips. "We are going to have so much fun."

I pull back and stand from the couch. "Let's go to bed."

She blinks up at me. "You're staying here?" Her voice betrays her, showing her eagerness.

"Of course I am." I scoff. What a ridiculous question.

"I was beginning to wonder if you ever sleep," she jokes before standing as she heads towards the stairs.

I hum noncommittally and trail behind her, a new buzzing sensation in my veins. Watching her sleep is one thing, and having sex is another, but sleeping next to one another is a new level of intimacy between us. We quickly get ready for bed—Danielle seems to hoard toiletries, so she has extra of everything a person could need—and slip under the covers. Danielle curls into me, her head on my chest, as our breathing synchronizes.

A thought crosses my mind then. "Will he be calling tonight?" I can't help the bite in my tone.

She stiffens. "I hope not. He stopped by my mom's recently. I'm not sure what his plans are anymore."

"I don't like the sound of that."

"He doesn't know where I live. He may have found my phone number, but he won't find me." It sounds like she's trying to convince herself more than she's trying to convince me.

"Danielle." My voice is gruff. "Nothing will ever happen to you. He will never bother you again."

"What're you going to do?" she asks.

"Whatever I need to." I'd happily kill him. If I brought him to Cherry, she'd dispose of him for me. She might get on my case a bit, but she'd do it.

She tilts her head to look up at me, her dark eyes wide. "Jesus, Blair, it's fine. You can't resort to murder, if that's what you're thinking."

"Why not?" I push.

"Because killing is wrong." Something in her voice sounds off, like she doesn't quite believe that. "This isn't very good pillow talk."

"No? Killing a man that harms you doesn't soothe you to sleep?" I caress her forearm that lays on my chest. "Tell me what a better topic of conversation would be."

"Maybe we shouldn't talk at all." She props herself up on her elbow, her gorgeous curls flowing down her shoulder. "Maybe we do something better with our mouths."

My blood heats at her words. I give her a sinister smile in answer. "What a great idea."

Chapter 31

Danielle

Blair's eyes blaze as she stares me down. "I know what you want."

"I seriously doubt that," I retort, but it comes out breathy.

Her eyebrows raise slightly. "You have a lot of fantasies." She winds her fingers in my hair and tugs as she sits up, towering over me.

"Those are between me and my books."

Her stormy eyes dip to my lips and back up. "I can help them come true."

My blood heats at the promise. "Oh?"

Other hand caressing the sides of my neck, my jaw, Blair murmurs, "Let me show you. Use your safe word if you want it to stop."

"Okay." My body winds itself tight with anticipation.

She pulls my head back so that I'm stuck. "You will do exactly what I say, when I say it. If you don't," she gives an evil grin, "you'll be punished."

"What, are you my Daddy or something?" I joke.

Blair tugs on my hair, causing prickles of pain to burst across my scalp. "Fuck yeah, I am." She roughly lets me go and gets off the bed, nearly giving me mental whiplash. "Strip."

I want to fight her on it, just to see what she'll do. Will she force me? Rip my clothes off herself? The thought of that makes me nearly pant with need.

I peel my clothes away from my body, feeling like my skin is on fire from the brand her stare is giving me. Her eyes trace over every curve, every scar, every dimple in my skin. She looks like she wants to eat me alive.

Licking her lips, she backs up until her legs hit the chair tucked into my desk, and she quickly drags it around and seats herself. "Get on your knees."

Nerves suddenly slither in my stomach.

Without thinking, I find myself getting off the bed and lowering into a kneel.

Blair gives me a small smile, and it nearly makes all of this worth it. "Crawl to me, Danielle."

Oh fuck, this is so humiliating. My skin feels hot as I get on my hands and knees and crawl over to her. I keep my eyes down on the floor, feeling a mixture of embarrassment and arousal. Once her feet come into view, I halt, unsure of what to do next.

Blair hums from above. "You like being told what to do, don't you?" I nod, worried my voice will betray the emotions warring in me. She continues, "And you like when I give you praise. Isn't that right?"

I nod again.

Suddenly, Blair leans forward and snatches my face, her fingers digging into my cheeks as she forces me to look at her.

"When I ask you a question, you respond appropriately. Don't just nod or shake your head; give me a verbal answer. Is that understood?"

I gulp. "Yes."

"Yes what?"

"Yes, Daddy."

She lets go of my cheeks and leans back. "Good." She moves one of her bare feet so it sits in front of me. "Kiss my foot."

I'm taken aback by the command. My public health mind is telling me how unsanitary—

"Do it," she snarls. Before I can chicken out, I lean down and press a kiss on her foot. "Very good," she praises, and those two words make arousal bloom in my stomach. "Kiss the other one." I do without hesitation. "Now sit down and grind on it."

Holy fuck. My core tightens at her words, at the demand. I've never done this before—I've never done anything like *this*. This is the kind of stuff you read about in smut books, but I never thought I'd get to do them.

I shift myself lower to ride on Blair's foot. I lift my gaze and get caught in the storm in her eyes. She lounges above me, a queen on her throne.

For some reason, it gives me the confidence to press myself against her and circle my hips. Pleasure warms my body—at the act, the feeling that this is taboo, at seeing Blair above me—as I grind my clit against her foot. I set my rhythm, desire quickly burning through me.

Blair doesn't take her eyes off me; they dart from my eyes to my lips, to my chest, to where we're touching, and back up again.

"Good girl," Blair murmurs. "Ride that foot."

A moan escapes me as I grind my hips faster and faster, chasing the high.

"Say you're mine."

Alarm bells go off in my head, but I can't pay attention to them through the haze of pleasure clouding me. "I'm yours."

A low growl emits from Blair's chest at my words. I realize in this moment that neither of us can get enough; we need more, we need it all. We're as bad as each other.

And that really turns me on.

Release gathers at my spine, ready to whisk me away. I don't even care how degrading this is. I think I'm actually enjoying how dirty it feels to do this. Soft whimpers fill the air as I keep going. My eyes close as I realize I'm actually going to come from this.

"Stop."

My eyes snap open. "What? No, I'm right there—"

Blair hinges forward and takes one of my nipples in between her fingers, pinching hard enough that pain jolts through me. I yelp and lean into her hand, hoping it will lessen the discomfort, but she has me in a vice.

"I told you to stop. That means you stop." She tugs on my nipple, making me cry out. "Do you understand?"

"Blair, it hurts," I whine.

She tugs again. "Do you understand me, you brat?"

"Fuck, yes, I understand, just let go!"

She releases me and I quickly cup my abused nipple. "You have a safe word, Danielle. Use it if you need to."

"I know," I whisper and hold her gaze.

I'm not using it. I don't want to. I want to see how far I can go, how far she can push me until I break. And even then, I want her to put me back together.

As if she can hear my thoughts, her eyes heat and she licks her lips. "You're perfect. I'm going to keep you and make sure you're mine forever."

Arousal lights my body up. This is so wrong, but maybe that's why I like it, why it's making me writhe with need.

"Stop," she demands again. Irritation builds in me, especially as she smirks down at me, like she knows exactly what she's doing. "I want a taste instead."

Before my mind can make sense of her words, she's pulling me by my hair as she stands and drags me to the bed. "Up on the bed."

I scramble up as soon as Blair releases my hair, my back hitting the mattress. "You're dripping down your legs," she snickers as she stares at my pussy, making me clench around nothing.

"I—" She kneels on the ground and starts feasting on me, making me grip the sheets to keep myself in my body. "Oh," I pant. Her tongue swirls expertly over my clit, and it feels so filthy, so wrong, but it feels too good to stop. I lose myself in the throes of lust. I'm already so worked up that it doesn't take long for me to reach the pinnacle. Her tongue is so soft and warm, I'll never feel anything as good ever again.

"I'm going to come," I moan to the ceiling, to her, to the world.

She chuckles against me. "Go on, then," she instructs.

I let go, release slamming into me as she laps me up like she loves my taste. My cries fill the room, and my hips ride her face with abandon. I can't even bring myself to be embarrassed by how desperate I am, by how loud I'm being. She works me through it, not letting up until my cries turn into sated whimpers.

Her tongue leaves me and I already miss the warmth.

I lift my head up and watch her lick her lips. "You taste like you were made for me."

A shiver works up my spine at her words. Before I can respond, she dives back in, her teeth lightly scraping my clit. My legs try to close, to stop her from causing pain, but she grabs my thighs and forces me wide.

"Don't you dare," she snarls, her stormy eyes lifting to mine, violence churning in them. But as she goes back to it, her teeth have been replaced by her tongue.

Even though I just came, I feel release gathering in me again. I whimper pitifully, letting my body ride the waves of pleasure as Blair pulls another orgasm from me.

She keeps her eyes on me, holding me hostage in them as I'm thrown into ecstasy, my body trembling. It's like she sucked my soul right out of my pussy.

When I come back down, Blair lifts her mouth from me, a feline grin on her face as she purrs, "Let's get you cleaned up."

"Wait," I whisper, unable to speak any louder. "I want to taste you, too."

Her stormy eyes soften a fraction. "I don't think you have it in you right now." She gestures to my boneless body spread across the mattress.

"Rude. But true," I sigh. "Next time," I mumble, my eyes shutting. I feel Blair get up, but I have no energy to react. A moment later, a warm washcloth presses against me and I settle back into the mattress, letting her care for me. I can't remember the last time I felt so relaxed.

Her warmth leaks into me as she settles into bed, and I'm asleep in moments.

Chapter 32

Danielle

Waking up next to Blair instead of waking up to her standing over me is something I could get used to.

I slept peacefully in her arms, not even needing my ear plugs and eye mask to stay asleep. It was so nice that I keep my eyes closed, just so I can stay here—safe, warm, no responsibilities or worries.

"I know you're awake," Blair's voice rumbles in my ear.

A smile darts across my lips but I don't open my eyes. "Hmm?"

"You nearly pushed me off the bed last night."

I furrow my brows and sit up, my eyes opening to see Blair nearly hanging off the side of the bed. "Oh, oops. Sorry. Why didn't you move me?"

"I did," she grumbles, her eyes churning. "No matter how many times I moved you, you kept coming right back."

My face gets hot. "I haven't slept next to someone in a while," I admit. "I've forgotten my manners."

"You have," she says in her no-nonsense way. She sits up and kisses my bare shoulder. "It was nice having you pressed against me all night."

Butterflies flutter in my stomach. "Do people like us tend to enjoy the sex we do?" I ask.

"They might, but," she pulls back to give me an evil smile, "I had some special insight into your desires."

I frown in confusion. "What do you mean?"

"I snuck a look at what books you enjoy reading." She *tsks* playfully. "Such a dirty girl."

My cheeks flame. "That's an invasion of privacy."

"I was curious. Being curious isn't wrong."

I groan, embarrassment burning my skin.

"There's nothing to be ashamed of," she tells me. "You fantasize about the same scenarios that I do. I will say, though, I was a bit perplexed by the common theme of submission in the stories. I assumed your past relationship would have tainted such an experience."

I swallow my chagrin and square my shoulders. I know there's nothing wrong or shameful reading books with erotica in them, and I don't feel ashamed. I shouldn't be shocked that she looked through my reading list, either.

"At first, I refused to be submissive during sex; I needed to be in control at all times, and I thought that meant not submitting to anyone. But as I started reading about it, I realized the submissive has most, if not all, of the power. So, as I learned more, I figured out that it could feel...good to submit, to let go. To trust someone so much that I can lose myself without fear of being hurt." I squirm in my skin a bit at the words that want to be spoken. "I never fully let go until I was with you." My eyes stay cast down to my hands sitting in my lap. "I think I use erotica to help me heal. I'm not sure if that makes sense."

I give a self-conscious chuckle. It feels like I just ripped my chest open for Blair to inspect—and to potentially reach in and rip my heart out.

We sit in awkward silence for a moment, making me feel even worse. "I shouldn't have said all that, I—"

Blair's fingers link through mine. "That makes perfect sense to me."

I peek up at her and see her scrutinizing me, a soft expression on her face. "It does?"

"Of course." Her mouth quirks to the side. "I've always wanted my sexual partners to enthusiastically consent. I don't need to coerce or force anyone."

"You would break into my house and watch me without my consent," I point out.

"First of all, I've never stalked anyone before you. And second, I don't force sexual partners to do anything they don't want to do. I find it boring and unnecessary, as there's always someone else out there who will want to do it."

All uncertainty I felt towards Blair evaporates. I could sense she would never force me to do something I didn't want to, but hearing it from her mouth solidifies that gut instinct.

I turn and lean into her, my muscles relaxing. "What's on the agenda for today?"

She hums against my skin, her lips tracing my neck. "Considering you threw away the cinnamon rolls I made for you—"

"You should've known I wasn't going to eat those—"

"—I'll have to try again." She buries her head in my lion's mane and takes a deep inhale.

"I don't think I have all the ingredients for that," I murmur. "I'm not much of a baker."

Her arms wind around my waist and she says into my hair, "We'll make do."

We did not, in fact, make do. I thought Blair's head was going to explode when she saw the measly baking rations in my kitchen cabinets. I offered to drive us to the store, but she waved me off and ordered everything she needed for grocery delivery.

"What can I help with?" I'd asked once all the ingredients had been received and spread across my kitchen counter.

"Just sit there and look pretty," she'd demanded, which was perfectly fine with me.

I sat at the island, sipping my coffee and watching Blair get lost in her task. Her look of concentration might be my favorite—eyebrows bunched, eyes zeroed in, mouth slightly open.

I know Blair doesn't wear her masks around me, but I like uncovering new versions of her. Even if they're apparently a foreign thing to her.

A few hours later, I'm shoveling cinnamon rolls into my mouth like there's no tomorrow.

"You're going to choke," Blair warns.

I shrug. "I'd happily die like this," I try to say, but it comes out jumbled around my food. She rolls her eyes, but a tiny smile plays on her lips.

"You like to bake." I state.

She nods. "Sometimes." As I take another bite, she takes a sip of her coffee and glances back toward my pantry. "I'm dismayed by the contents of your kitchen. How do you live like this?"

I swallow. "I don't really bake. The flours are too difficult to work with when they don't have gluten to bind it together."

"Hm. And I assume you don't eat out much."

"Not really. It can be too risky. I can tell a restaurant that I'm gluten free, but I don't know how seriously they take cross-contamination." I shake my head. "I don't really want to pay money just to get sick."

Blair scrutinizes me for a moment before saying, "I need to make a call." She stands abruptly from her seat and marches out of the kitchen.

My eyes follow her, but I just shrug. It's not the first time I've not understood Blair's behavior.

I get up to feed my fish, who is lounging underneath his plants. "She's a bit of an odd one," I tell him before sprinkling in his food.

About twenty minutes later, Blair is demanding I get dressed, and that she'll be back to get me. When I press her, she simply says, "We're going on a date," before disappearing.

Chapter 33
Danielle

As I sit in my car that she's driving, dressed in a cream knit sweater, a plaid skirt with tights and knee-high boots, I worry that I'm wearing the wrong thing.

"You can't even tell me where we're going?" I ask for the thousandth time.

"So impatient," she murmurs. She jerks her chin to a building in the distance. "It's right there."

We pull up in front of a small restaurant named Forked Tongues. Unease tightens my stomach. "I haven't looked this place up on my Gluten Free app." I go to fish my phone out of my purse. "Just give me one second to look at their reviews."

"No need," Blair says as she pulls into a parking spot out front. "I've done my research."

I chew on my bottom lip as I look over at her. "I believe you, but there's other things to consider, like—"

"Like cross-contamination," she finishes for me. "Yes, I know. Don't worry, sweetheart, I've taken care of everything."

With that, she opens her door and steps out, quickly gliding over to my door and opening it for me. She extends her hand, which I hesitantly place my own into. My food anxiety is trying to climb up my throat, telling me that I'll get sick, that this place won't take my illness seriously, that—

Blair keeps a hold on my hand as she shuts the car door and gently forces me to lean against the cool exterior, barricading me in. Her gray eyes ensnare mine, refusing to let me go.

"I called them to discuss their kitchen preparedness when it comes to allergens. We discussed their extensive gluten free menu and how they prepare everything separately, but they could not ensure it was celiac-safe during a regular day. So, I paid them to close down the restaurant for us."

I blink. "You did what?"

"If there's no one else ordering food from them, they have no need to handle wheat or other food with gluten in them." She shrugs. "The only ones patronizing this establishment tonight is us."

And just like that, my anxiety dissipates. "I can't believe you did that for me," I murmur, a well of emotions coming to the surface.

She tilts her head, scrutinizing me. "Have I upset you?"

I let out a small, bemused laugh. "No, no. You've done quite the opposite, actually."

Even though Blair is supposed to help me see what emotions are real and what are masks, this feeling is definitely real. She's starting to make me feel like I'm the only person in the world, like we're meant to have everything we've ever wanted. Like we're supposed to go through life together.

That is a feeling I want to feel every second.

The corner of her mouth quirks. She nods, as if registering my emotions and what they mean, before pulling back and walking us to the restaurant's entrance.

Forked Tongues is small, with only thirty or so tables spread throughout the space. The hostess stand is off to the left, with the tables set up to the right. There's nothing separating us from the kitchen, where staff move about the space, large ovens at their backs.

The hostess smiles at us. "Welcome, Mrs. and Mrs. Erickson. I'll show you to your table." She grabs two menus and guides us through.

"Mrs. Erickson?" I mutter to Blair as we follow.

She glances down at me, her eyebrows raised in challenge.

"You didn't correct her," she points out.

We pass the open kitchen, the sound of the news from a small TV reporting on the recent murders reaching our ears.

I roll my eyes just as the hostess finishes placing the menus on the table and turns to us with a smile. "Your server will be out shortly."

"Thank you," I tell her, giving her a smile before she heads back up front. Blair pulls out my seat for me then sitting in her own.

"I only want to be called someone else's last name if I have a giant rock on my finger," I joke, holding up my left hand and wiggling my fingers.

Blair's eyes blaze as she leans back in her chair. "You will not have *someone else's* name—you will have mine. And as for the ring, that is being sorted as we speak."

I shake my head. "You aren't being serious."

"Have I ever joked when it comes to you?"

"You don't get to marry me simply because you want to," I argue. "We both have to want that."

Her answering smile is dazzling. "I'm willing to wait as long as I need to."

Butterflies flutter around in my stomach. I'm not right in the head for liking this. "Don't waste your time on a ring. You don't even know what I like, or even what my ring size is."

She pins me with a look—a look that peels back the curtain to the danger that lurks under the surface. A thrill runs up my spine. Yeah, I'm definitely fucked up. "I had ample opportunities to find out the necessary information."

It takes me a moment for her words to register. "You measured my ring size while I was sleeping?"

Blair shrugs, giving me the answer. At this point, I shouldn't be surprised by her actions.

I pivot the conversation to something else. "So, you like baking. What else do you like?"

She tilts her head. "I like you."

I roll my eyes. "Doesn't count. I meant, what other hobbies do you have?"

"Does fucking you count as a hobby?"

"No." My cheeks heat at her vulgar words spoken in public. "Take me out of the equation."

She purses her lips in thought. "I enjoy drawing," she answers after a while.

I blink. "Really?"

"Is that hard to believe?"

"Yeah, kinda," I admit. "What do you draw?"

She shrugs. "Things I enjoy. What do you like to do?"

Her question makes me pause. Part of me doesn't want to be honest. "I don't really do anything. When I get home, I just...sit around. I like to read, I guess."

She chuckles. "I know. I perused your collection."

I roll my eyes. "You're impossible." I pick up my napkin and begin fanning myself with it, hoping it'll cool me down from the searing embarrassment that radiates through my face.

"Like I told you, there's nothing to be ashamed of. I was impressed by your wide range of interests."

"Shut up," I grumble.

The server comes over, takes our orders, and leaves us be.

"So," Blair starts. "I want to know everything about this ex that won't leave you alone."

I nearly spit my wine out. "What? Why?"

"I want to know what he's done, so I can make sure he pays for it."

"Blair, please, I really don't—"

"I don't like how he speaks to you," she growls, her nostrils flaring. "He should have his tongue removed for that."

"You're right," I agree, startling myself. I take a steadying breath. "But he's in the past. Isn't that enough?"

"He isn't," she argues. "He still haunts you, Danielle."

"Can we talk about literally anything else? I don't want to lose my appetite."

"I want to know."

"Well, it isn't up to you," I sneer. "What happened to me, what he did to me, is something I should share when I'm ready. If I don't want to share it at a dinner that was romantic up until thirty seconds ago, then I don't fucking have to."

Blair blinks, her only show of surprise. "You're right," she admits. "I didn't think about it that way."

I snort, my irritation simmering under the surface.

"I thought sharing would lessen the burden."

I fight to keep myself in check and not blow my lid. "It's okay."

She shakes her head. "It isn't. I apologize."

Now it's my turn to blink in surprise. "Oh. Thank you."

"What?" Her gray eyes bounce around my face, trying to read me.

"I just...didn't expect you to apologize." I shrug. "You just don't seem like the type."

"I'm not," she answers. "But you said we could learn things from one another. I want to learn how to be there for you in a way you'll receive."

She's taking this way better than anticipated.

"It's fine." I take a healthy gulp of my wine, setting the glass down gently. "Let's talk about something else. Tell me about your sister."

Blair's eyebrows quirk a fraction, but her expression evens out quickly. "Where do I even begin with her?" she sighs, mostly to herself, the previous conversation seemingly forgotten.

Chapter 34
Danielle

Blair nearly has to roll me out of the restaurant from all the food I ate. I feel positively sated, rubbing my stomach as Blair drives us back to my house.

"Thank you for doing that. I won't need to eat for a few days now."

She snorts. "You inhaled your food."

"I did," I sigh contentedly. "Are you staying over again tonight?"

"Of course. I'm not even sure why you would ask."

I roll my eyes. "What would you like to do?"

"I could show you my sketchbook," she offers, surprising me.

"Really?"

"If you would like to see it." She pulls into my driveway and shuts off the car before turning to me. "I've never showed anyone my art. But you're not just anyone."

My breath catches in my throat. "Oh," is all I manage to say.

Her mouth quirks before she climbs out of the car and heads to the trunk. I step out into the dark and cold winter night just as Blair is pulling a black duffel bag from the back. I blink in surprise. When did she put that in the trunk of my car?

Silently, she walks to me and takes my hand, leading me into the house.

We shuck off our winter gear and gravitate towards the living room couch. "You don't have to share if you don't want to," I tell her, the conversation at the restaurant coming to the forefront of my mind.

"I know." She sits next to me and unzips her bag, pulling out her sketchbook. "I realized it's unfair to expect you to be vulnerable when I haven't been. I guess I'm showing you this because I want you to feel..." She cocks her head, as if searching for the right word. "Safe with me."

My heart squeezes. "Okay."

Blair hands me the sketchbook, and I flip it open to the first page.

Then the next.

And the one after that.

"Blair," I gasp, emotions clogging my throat. "Is this...?"

"It is," she murmurs.

Drawings of me are splashed on every page; me sleeping, me at my work desk, me in my kitchen.

All art of me.

Some are realistic portraits, while others are more abstract interpretations. One is my body, but my head has been replaced with a galaxy of stars, asteroids, and planets. Another is of me sitting down, staring directly ahead with a dark shadow lurking behind me, its hand on my shoulder.

My fingers gently stroke my face on the page, mesmerized.

"These are beautiful," I whisper, entranced.

"Thank you," Blair rumbles next to me. "I told you I draw things I enjoy."

I let out a huff of a laugh. "You did." I drag my eyes away from the pages and blurt out, "Will you draw me right now?"

Blair blinks. "You want to pose for me?"

I nod, excitement swirling in my veins. "Right here." I pat the couch. "Does that work for you?"

She looks around the room. "The lighting isn't ideal—"

"I have a shit ton of candles," I interrupt, realizing how much I want this. How badly I want to experience this with her. I'm sure I sound desperate, but I'm past caring.

Blair's eyes soften a fraction. "That would be perfect."

Over a dozen candles light my living room, giving it a warm, welcoming glow. Blair has pushed my coffee table against the wall and positioned a chair across from the couch.

"Are you ready?" she asks, her sketchbook in her lap and charcoal in her hand.

"I am," I say, confidently standing here in my robe. With nothing on underneath.

Slowly, my fingers lift and tug on the ribbon. The robe peeks open, giving Blair a taste before I sensually slip it off and let it pool at my feet.

I've been naked in front of her before, but not like this.

Her eyes travel down my body, drinking me in, hunger swirling in her eyes. "On the couch." Her voice comes out as a near growl.

I obey, loving how much I affect her. How she can barely control herself, but would keep herself leashed if I demanded it.

I position myself on the couch, laying down like Rose did in *Titanic*. All that I'm missing is a massive jewel around my neck. "Is this good?"

Blair looks ready to launch herself at me, but she nods. "It's perfect."

With that, she opens her sketchbook and begins.

Her face quickly shifts to that look of concentration I saw earlier, her eyes darting from me to the page and back again. I hold still, enjoying this time to get my fill of her in her element. It's as if we've entered a different world, where it's just me and her. The thread connecting us is taut, as if pulling us closer so we'll never be apart.

This may be the most intimate thing I've done with anyone.

My mind drifts back to the argument we had just a few hours ago. I was right in telling her off, and I'm glad she backed down. Up until now, part of me wanted to hold back, to not let Blair see the deepest and darkest parts of myself.

I realize it's not even about Blair; it's about me. I know Blair would never make me feel ashamed for what I've gone through, but I *do* feel shame. Shame for not leaving the first time he put his hands on me, for taking so long to be free of him.

Logically, I know it isn't my fault, but that ugly, nasty part of me wants me to think it was.

I'm tired of being controlled by my shame.

I'll share with her, I decide. I'll share with her and finally—hopefully—release it.

Chapter 35

Blair

I'm mesmerized by the woman before me.

Danielle's beautiful body is on display, her hair framing her soft face like a halo. Her siren song begs me to come forward, to capture her and never let her go.

The charcoal moves across the paper almost by second nature as it depicts her curves, her large eyes, the dimple on her cheek. I've drawn her time and again, so often that I can visualize her perfectly.

I add the final touches and catch her studying me. "Would you like to see?"

She licks her lips and slowly gets up from the couch, padding over to me. My mouth waters as I unabashedly watch her approach. I turn the sketchbook to face her, and she gasps.

"Blair," she whispers, her eyes glued to my art. "That's really me?"

It's like she can't believe that she's this stunning creature. "It is."

She swallows before murmuring, "It's beautiful. Can I...can I keep it?"

Something in my chest tenses. Is my heart suddenly beating abnormally fast? "Of course," I push out.

Danielle's dimple appears as she smiles softly. "Thank you. You're very talented."

I grunt, trying to figure out what just happened to me. Maybe I should see a doctor.

"Can we talk about something?"

Her words snap me from my thoughts. I tilt my head. "What is it?"

She shuffles away and picks her robe off the floor, quickly throwing it around herself. "I was thinking about the restaurant—what you wanted me to share. I realized that," she takes a deep breath, "I should share what happened. If you're still open to listening."

I thought we just talked about this. "You don't have to, Danielle. Really."

She shakes her head. "I know. I want to."

I study her for a moment, gauging how honest she's being. Anxiety rolls off her in waves, but her eyes are open, vulnerable.

I nod. "All right. Let me wash up first." I hold up my charcoal-stained hands.

She gives me a relieved smile in reply.

I rush to the bathroom, washing my hands in a hurry so that I don't give Danielle time to change her mind.

Yes, I want her to share this with me because I think it will be good for her, but I also want to know for my own selfish reasons.

I want to know how much pain I should inflict upon him before I kill him.

Danielle tells me that isn't what she wants, but it's what *I* want. It's the least he deserves. The world will be a better place without him.

I race into the living room to find Danielle on the couch, her feet curled underneath her. Sitting next to her, she gives me a nervous look before her eyes drop to her lap.

"Jeremy and I met in college, at a frat party one night," she begins. "I was a freshman and grew up relatively sheltered, so I didn't know what to expect. He was a junior, clearly the life of the party. As soon as my friends and I arrived, someone shoved a red solo cup full of something into my hand. I still don't know what it was, but it tasted awful." Her nose wrinkles as if remembering the taste. "My friends drifted off, and I was left alone in the corner, nursing this gross drink, when he came up to me.

"He was tall and muscular and had deep green eyes. He gave me an award-winning smile and asked if I wanted to be his beer pong partner. I thought he was joking, so I just smiled politely and told him 'no thanks,' but he took my hand and led me into the kitchen, where the game was happening. I was shit at beer pong, but he didn't seem phased by us losing. After the game, he took me to the backyard for some fresh air, and he told me I was the most beautiful girl he'd seen at this school.

"I couldn't believe this older guy—this older, cute, popular guy—wanted to spend time with me. So, when he leaned in to kiss me, I kissed him back. We were inseparable after that moment.

"I mistook his controlling tendencies for care; when he demanded we be in almost all the same classes, even though I was two years younger, or when he made me outline my work schedule so he'd know when to drop me off and pick me up. I was always at his place—he didn't like staying at mine because he said my roommates were rude to him."

She shakes her head. "I think it's because my father was the same way with my mother. If he hit her, I never saw it, but they would spend weeks pretending like everything was okay, even though it clearly wasn't. I didn't realize that I was just mirroring my parents' relationship.

"The first time he hit me was the night of my graduation." White-hot fury burns in me. "We were driving to my celebratory dinner, and we got into an argument. I don't even remember what we were arguing about now, but it led to him slamming my head against the window. My vision went blurry, and my ears were ringing. I was in shock, I couldn't believe he'd put his hands on me like that. He pulled the car over and started crying, telling me how sorry he was, and he didn't mean to, that it would never happen again. I told him it was all right, but I was too afraid to say that I thought otherwise.

"We had dinner with my parents, and he was his regular charming self, was doting on me all evening afterwards. It made me wonder if it had even happened, that maybe I'd imagined it."

She lets out a shaky breath. "It got worse after we moved in together, but we were in a cycle: he'd hurt me, then apologize and would say he'd get better, and then we'd have a few weeks or even months of happy times...until he'd hurt me again.

"It got so bad, I'd have to miss work because I'd be covered in bruises, or I'd need a cast put on a broken bone. He was getting more violent, and the good times were happening less and less. He loved belittling me, telling me I'd never get anywhere without him." A hollow laugh escapes her throat. "I believed it—that I deserved the beatings, that no one would ever love me, that I was worthless."

My entire body is on fire with my rage.

"Then, one day, I sensed something...off. He came home from work, and his eyes..." She shudders. "I don't know how to explain it, but it was like they were...dead. That's when I knew I had to get out. If I didn't, I knew he'd kill me. I wasn't sure who to call—he'd done a great job at isolating me—but I called my college roommates on a whim, and they jumped into action. I stayed at Lacy's while I got everything in order: job transfer, new phone number, new everything.

"Still, part of me was scared to leave—to really, truly *live*. He destroyed any sense of self-worth I had. I would never find someone who would love me, who would see me as anything other than a useless mess." Her eyes squeeze shut. "But once I found out he cheated on me, it was like whatever hold he had on me broke. It was one thing to hurt me, control me, and not let me live without fear, but then to fuck someone else?"

Her eyes open and land on me, the predator beneath the surface staring back at me. "I lived in fear for months, hiding where I lived, who I talked to. I became a hermit. It took me years of therapy to realize I was safe from him.

"Until a few months ago. He started showing up at my work, calling my friends, my family. I didn't know what to do. Why was he showing up after all this time?"

I answer, "Once a killer has their target, they struggle with letting them go."

She nods as if she's familiar. "Exactly. That's when I realized I had to move. He wasn't going to let me live there anymore. So, I packed up my life and moved here. Only my two friends that got me out know where I am."

I blink. "Your family doesn't know?"

She shakes her head, her eyes sad. "My parents loved Jeremy. I told my mother I'd called off the wedding, and she told me I was making a terrible mistake. I didn't have the heart to tell her the truth."

I fight the urge to get up and find every single person that has upset her and make sure their ends are excruciatingly painful.

Danielle sighs. "He hasn't found me here, but he managed to get my new phone number. I'm not sure how, but I assume my mother gave it to him."

My teeth grind as my mind replays the vitriol I heard him spew over the phone at her. "I assume you keep them for evidence against him, in case anything happens to you." Her eyes are bleak as she nods. "I'm going to kill him," I promise.

"Blair," she sighs.

"No," I growl. "I won't hear it. He is still a threat to you. Nothing is going to happen to you, but I need to get rid of any threats."

"This isn't up for discussion."

"You're right."

"That doesn't mean you can kill him," she says slowly.

"Yes, it does."

Her eyes grow exasperated. "I don't even know why we're arguing about this."

"I don't either." I reach over and take her hand, my chest constricting in that strange, new way again. I push past it and say, "Let me do this. Let me hurt him for what he's done to you. Let me make him wish for death. I will gladly lay his head at your feet so that you may finally heal. Please, let me do this for you."

She holds my gaze for a few moments, the air charged between us. "I'll think about it," she says finally.

My chest eases with relief. It's a step in the right direction.

But I'm still going to kill him, regardless.

Chapter 36
Blair

Winter has descended on us, gifting us with snow nearly every night. Thanksgiving has come and gone, and barely anyone is plugged into work. They're all too busy thinking about their upcoming vacations.

Meaning I can fuck Danielle in my office with no distractions.

She comes up to see me every day, a devious grin on her lips before I bend her over my desk and bring her to orgasm again and again. My favorite day was when I had her on my lap, playing with her as I sat in a Zoom call. My video was off, but my microphone was not, so my other hand clapped over her mouth as she came all over me while the team discussed analytics of the newest advertisements.

But today, she walks in with a sheepish look on her face. "Are you busy?"

I lean back in my chair, my eyes dragging up and down her body. My chest is doing that strange constricting thing—in fact, it seems to be doing it every time I see her.

At times, this sensation is even accompanied by a feeling of warmth spreading through my body.

It's the strangest thing.

I went to see Cherry's hot-shot son who is also a doctor, and he confirmed everything is fine. I'm not so convinced.

"Not for you."

She sits across from me, tucking a curl behind her ear. "My college friends are coming to visit me. It's a short notice thing—they told me that flights were cheap, and they wanted to take some time off before the holidays." She rubs her hands on her thighs. "I haven't even told them about you."

"Well, tell them," I say, not really sure where she's going with this.

"It's not that simple," she argues. "They're very protective of me—"

"So am I. We'll have that in common."

"They got me out of that relationship. I worry they won't take to anyone I date because they're worried."

"I'll be on my best behavior," I promise.

She groans. "No, you won't."

"You're right, I probably won't." I drum my fingers on the desk. "When do they get here?"

"They fly in Friday, which means I only have two days to get my guest bedroom in order." She huffs.

I give her a lopsided grin. "I can help you with that. Now, come over here and forget your worries for a moment."

She rolls her eyes but rises from her chair and rounds the desk. I push my chair back to let her sit on my lap.

"It'll be fine," I offer as my arms wind around her waist. "Just tell them how well I take care of you."

Leaning in, she brushes her nose against mine. "I doubt they'd want all those gory details."

A laugh vibrates in my chest. "Maybe not."

I meet her halfway, our lips connecting. Lightning strikes my body as we come together, our mouths opening to explore one another. Our tongues dance as we get our fill.

"Now," I whisper, pulling back slightly. "Be my good little girl and sit on my desk."

Chapter 37
Danielle

"We just landed!" Lacy shouts through the phone.

"How was the flight? Did Kristina have a panic attack?"

"I made sure she took her Xanax before we got to the airport. She was only slightly terrified this time."

"You're sure you don't need me to pick you up?" I ask for what feels like the millionth time.

"Nah, we didn't want to die today, so we're taking an Uber," she teases. "We should be to you in an hour. We're excited to see you and your fancy new digs."

I snort. "See you soon. Just let yourselves in when you get here."

"Your security system won't shoot us when we approach your door, will it?"

"I've turned that feature off," I joke before we hang up.

My closest—and only—friends are staying with me for a few days. Truthfully, they've been badgering me to let them come out here, but I've been a bit distracted. Mostly with the woman who was in my bed earlier this morning.

Blair made it clear she'd like to meet them, and the thought gave me butterflies. But now, I sit in my living room, biting my nails over it. I already know I can't be honest with them.

What am I going to say? *Hey, so I've started seeing someone new, but don't worry, she's nothing like Jeremy. Oh, how did we meet? She actually repeatedly broke into my home and watched me sleep.*

Yeah, that won't go over well.

I know Blair puts on a convincing mask when interacting with others, but something about it nags at me. Seeing this fake version of her that's used to be digestible for people has started to make my skin crawl the more I see it.

This must be how Blair felt about me when we first met.

Sighing, I get up and head into the kitchen to feed Swim Shady. He swims to the top of the tank eagerly, ready for his fish food. I sprinkle some in and watch him try to eat them before they sink to the bottom.

"Huh," I say as I inspect him. "You seem rounder." His little fish stomach is slightly wider than the rest of him. I didn't think I was overfeeding him. "Maybe we need to cut back a bit."

I spend the next fifty-eight minutes anxiously tidying up. I'm lost in reorganizing my fridge when I hear, "Hello!"

Slamming the fridge shut and racing for the door, I'm greeted by Kristina and Lacy. They're decked out in their winter gear and are dragging small suitcases behind them. They both squeal when they see me and rush forward, gathering me up in a group hug. I have to fight my body's response to clam up, forcing myself to relax in the embrace.

"Ugh, your house is so cute," Lacy gushes as we pull away.

"You've barely seen any of it." I roll my eyes playfully.

"Well, I love what I've seen already. We do need to get you some crystals, though."

"Let's at least take our shoes off before you start doing any magic," Kristina laughs, shrugging off her coat.

Kristina and Lacy could not be any more different than one another. Lacy's bohemian, go-with-the-flow vibe is perfectly accentuated by her white-blonde lion's mane that is rarely contained, her tattoo-covered arms, and multiple necklaces that clang together as she moves.

Kristina, on the other hand, looks like the epitome of a put-together woman. Her deep red hair is always blow-dried, makeup perfectly applied, and there's never a wrinkle in her clothes. She has no blemishes or imperfections or scars. It's a medical mystery.

I usher them in, getting them out of their coats and boots to begin the house tour. They *ooh* and *aah* when appropriate, peering under my bathroom cabinets and in my closets simply because they're nosy.

We end the tour in the living room, where I've laid out a plate of assorted cheeses and meats, with fruits and veggies on a separate dish, and a bottle of wine.

Lacy sighs contently when she sees the spread. "I know I can count on you to take my dietary needs seriously, Danielle." She plops on the couch and grabs a strawberry.

"Hey, I do too," Kristina scoffs as she sits down next to her.

"Yeah, but Danielle just gets it because she's on a special diet, too." Her words are muffled around the fruit.

"Danielle's diet is medically necessary; yours isn't."

"Being vegan is good for you, though."

The two continue to playfully poke at each other while I grab a piece of cheese, parking myself in the chair across from them. "So, what do you want to do while you're here?"

They look at me, then at each other, like they're having a silent conversation. These two have always been attached at the hip. I don't think they realize that they alienate others around them when they have these moments, though it never really bothered me. I was happy to be a third wheel.

Still, something about them seems different this time.

"We're down to do whatever," Lacy says, looking back at me. "Take us to your favorite place."

"Honestly, I spend a lot of time at home," I admit. My friends look at each other again. Eyebrows raising, I ask, "Is there something you need to tell me?"

Their eyes snap back to me, Lacy's are wild with faux innocence while Kristina's are guarded.

"No, of course not," Lacy laughs. "Why do you ask?"

"Because you two are acting weirder than usual." I gesture to them nearly sitting on top of one another.

Lacy sneaks a glance at Kristina. "Maybe we should just tell her."

They hold eyes for a moment, secretly conversing, before Kristina turns to me and blurts, "Lacy and I are together."

My eyes dart back and forth between them. "Like...?"

"Like we've been more than friends for a little bit," Lacy answers.

"Oh." I give them a wide smile. "Well, that's great, right?"

"Yes, of course it is." Kristina lets out a relieved sigh. "We were nervous to tell you because we didn't want things to be weird or to make you feel like a third wheel—"

"I'm already a third wheel here," I laugh. "If you two are happy, then I'm happy."

They hold each other's gazes, both grinning like lovesick puppies before Kristina murmurs, "Yeah, we're happy."

"Tell me everything," I nudge. "How did it happen?"

They launch into the story, their hands intertwining as they share how their love blossomed from a friendship into something more. They're taking things slow, as Kristina isn't out to her parents; she knows they won't disown her or anything like that, but she can't shake the anxiety that comes with coming out.

"Have you talked to your mom at all?" Lacy asks once they've filled me in.

I shake my head. "Not since the whole security system thing."

Kristina purses her lips. "Oh yeah, you never told us what that was about. I'm guessing it was your mom who got it for you?"

Shit. "Oh." A nervous laugh builds in my throat. "Uh, well, it was actually from someone I'm seeing."

They both freeze, their eyes going wide.

"Excuse me?" Kristina's tone is her no-nonsense one.

My hands feel clammy. "Yeah, it's a funny story—or, well, it's not really funny—"

"Who is this person?" Lacy's voice is ice cold.

"It's okay," I soothe, holding my palms up. "Blair is nothing like Jeremy."

"We'll be the judge of that." Kristina's expression brokers no argument.

"She'd like to meet you," I offer, hoping it'll ease the protective guard dog that lives in both these women. "I mean it, she wants nothing more than to protect me."

My friends spend the next several minutes grilling me, asking if Blair has exhibited any signs of possessiveness or controlling behavior Jeremy did.

I find myself struggling to answer the questions because she *has* been possessive and controlling, but in a completely different way. Jeremy didn't want me to have a life outside of him; Blair made it clear she wanted me to see my friends, and even wants to meet them.

I'm not afraid of Blair—at least, not anymore. When she tells me she won't hurt me, I believe her. She's never shown any violent tendencies. Sure, breaking into my house and stalking me is criminal, but...the thrill was exciting.

Lacy's eyes fill with tears as she whispers, "We're just concerned. We never want what happened with Jeremy to happen again."

My chest aches a bit at their worry. "I don't either. It won't." *I'm sure of it.*

"We have to meet her," Kristina declares.

"She'd love that," I tell them, which seems to settle their nerves.

The evening passes quickly, marked by laughing so hard we can't breathe and a few glasses of wine. Eventually, I yawn, and we pick ourselves up, heading upstairs to the bedrooms.

"Ugh, does this mean you'll be having sex in my guest bed?" I wrinkle my nose.

"No!" Kristina gasps just as Lacy says, "Oh, definitely."

Blair is meeting us at this coffee shop downtown, and I feel like I'm going to throw up from anxiety. My friends sit on either side of me, an impenetrable wall, ready to barricade me in if they don't like her.

I barely register that Kristina is speaking to me until Lacy nudges my arm. "Sorry, what?"

Looking over at Kristina, she's buried in her phone, face contorted with worry. "I asked if you've heard about all these murders in town. It sounds like men around the same age are disappearing—no bodies have been found, but they're presumed dead." Her eyes raise from her screen to my face. "Are you sure you're safe living here on your own?"

I snort. "Doesn't sound like I'm the killer's type."

"I'm serious."

"I know you are." I wave my hand dismissively, eager to change the subject. On the other side of me, Lacy has stopped paying attention, too busy taking aesthetic photos of her coffee to post online later. "I'm totally fine. Fancy new security system, remember?"

Kristina doesn't seem convinced, but she goes back to her phone.

The energy in the room shifts, alerting me to Blair's presence.

My eyes immediately find her, and I can't stop the smile that spreads across my face. Her glossy dark hair swishes as she strides towards us, her gray eyes alight in a way that makes it clear the mask is firmly in place.

My smile falters.

"Danielle," she greets me, giving me a peck on the cheek before turning to Kristina and Lacy. "I'm so happy to meet you both. I've heard such wonderful things."

I twist to look at both my friends as Blair sits across from us. My friends are eyeing her warily but there's a hint of curiosity underneath.

"Blair, is it?" Kristina asks in a clipped tone.

I roll my eyes.

Blair gives her a dazzling smile as she settles into the chair. "That's right. I'm glad we could make this happen."

"What do you want with Danielle?" Lacy shoots.

The smile on Blair's face doesn't crack. "I can assure you, there's nothing nefarious going on here. When I met Danielle, I was transfixed." Her eyes ensnare mine. "I've never met anyone like her. She's intelligent, sexy, a firecracker," she chuckles before her eyes grow serious. The rest of the world fades away, leaving just the two of us. She drops the mask for a moment, as if to show me that she means every word. "She's been through hell and clawed her way out. Danielle is resilient and beautiful and courageous. I feel honored that she wants me, and all I want is to cherish and protect her."

I suck in a breath as I bring myself out of her stormy eyes. Glancing over to my friends, I see that they're moved by her words.

That's when I realize I hate the mask she wears.

I hate that she has to hide who she is, that she needs to put it on because she needs to be digestible for the world.

I want to tear it from her skin and shield her from anyone who demands she wear it.

Blair and my friends are holding a conversation, but I can't even pay attention; I'm too busy trying to control my rage at how unfair this feels.

I love Blair for who she is, unhinged, possessive behavior included. I place my hand on her knee under the table, trying to show her that I see her; I see all of her, and I love her for it.

She places her hand on mine and squeezes my fingers in return.

Chapter 38
Danielle

The rest of the weekend moves in a blur. I'll be honest, I was *very* ready for my friends to leave by the time Sunday rolled around. It was nice to see them, but I desperately wanted to get back to my routine.

And back to Blair.

My friends were highly impressed after meeting her. "The way she looked at you, Danielle." Lacy began fanning herself after Blair left the coffee shop. "I'm gonna need a cold shower after that."

After they gave their stamp of approval, my friends seemed to relax. I didn't invite Blair to anything else with us this weekend because I couldn't stomach seeing that version of her. It felt just...wrong.

"We'll let you know once we get to the airport," Kristina tells me as all three of us gather into another group hug by my front door.

"You better," I tease before letting go. "And take your Xanax. You know how anxious flying makes you."

"Yeah, yeah." Kristina waves her hand dismissively as Lacy gives me a knowing look that says, *I'm on it.*

"Danielle, I just wanna say..." Lacy grabs my hands. "I'm so happy to see you doing well. You deserve all the good things the universe has in store for you."

"Uh huh," I grin, and she squeezes my hands.

"She's serious," Kristina adds. "I'm happy, too. I know you won't come back to visit, but we'll be back here soon." Her smile lights up her face before her phone pings.

"Oh, Uber's here!" They gather their bags and shuffle out the door. "We'll call you!"

I wave them off, watching them load their bags and then themselves into the car, and drive off.

~

The steam from the shower clouds my vision, but I can feel her presence. I'm not sure where she is, but I know she's somewhere, watching me.

I shut the water off and step out to find Blair leaning against the bathroom door frame. She smirks as I wrap myself in a towel. "Ending the show early?"

"I hated that," I blurt out, the words tumbling out. "I hate how you have to wear a mask around my friends—around anyone. It isn't fair."

She crosses her arms. "It doesn't bother me."

"But it bothers *me*. That version of you isn't who you really are."

"The masks we wear allow us freedom to live as we choose."

"But at what cost?" I walk over to her, my wet hair sticking to my neck, my shoulders. "I love who you are underneath. I don't want you to hide from me, and I won't hide from you either."

She looks at a loss for words. "You love me?" Her voice is so small, it cracks my heart.

"Who you really are—even though I was afraid at first—is who I want. I don't want the show you put on for everyone else."

A storm passes through her eyes as she stares down at me, showing me emotions I've never seen her portray.

Suddenly, she pushes off the door frame and turns her back to me. "I can't do this."

Chapter 39

Blair

I'm losing my mind. I feel stripped bare.

That constricting feeling is back. I must be having a heart attack. Cherry's son must be a quack who can't see I'm on death's door.

"What?" Danielle asks.

I can't do this. I can't let this woman, despite her own demons, care for me in such an...intimate way. It makes me feel like she's broken through all these walls and can see who I truly am, and isn't disgusted or horrified.

She needs to be.

"Blair." Danielle's soft hand lands on my shoulder. "It's okay."

"No," I grit out, "It's not okay. I've never felt this way before. This isn't normal—this *can't* be normal."

She walks around until she's standing in front of me. My heart is beating out of my chest.

Her bottomless dark eyes peer up at me, open and understanding. "What do you feel?"

My body buzzes with electricity. "I feel..." I struggle to put the sensations into words. "I feel...warm."

"Yes," she breathes, her eyes searching mine, encouraging me.

I push the words out. "When I look at you, I feel like I'm in pain. Like I'm slowly dying."

Her breath catches as she whispers, "I look at you and feel like I'm on fire. Like I'm burning up from the inside and I don't want it to stop."

"Exactly," I murmur, my eyes dipping to the column of her throat, down to her clavicles. Her skin has started to flush, and I drink it in greedily. "I never want to be away from you."

She swallows, her throat bobbing with the movement. My fingers lift and trail them down her neck, as if to feel her body working, to be one with her.

"I *can't* be away from you," she admits, leaning into my touch as my fingers skim her collarbones. "It's like I'm under some sort of spell that I never want to be lifted."

A groan builds in my chest. God, this woman.

"What is this?" I ask hoarsely. "How do I make it stop?"

That makes Danielle laugh, her body thrumming with the movement. "You don't. You just feel it."

"It's horrible," I admit. "Feeling is horrible."

"It can be." She reaches up to cup my face, gently touching my cheeks, my lips. "But it doesn't have to be. We can burn together."

"Yes." It's all I can voice before she kisses me softly, irreverently.

It's more intimate than what we've done before. It feels like every ugly and horrifying thing I've done is on full display and she accepts what she sees. I wrap my arms around her shoulders and press her against me—I need her closer, as close as possible.

She melts into me, our lips connected, our bodies flush together. Her warmth seeps into me as I lightly bite her bottom lip. A small whimper comes from her, and it spurs me on. The kiss becomes urgent, hungry, like we never want it to end. She's breathing life into me and I'm happily sucking it down.

My hands stroke down her back, grabbing at her towel. We break apart so I can rip it from her. My eyes fly open to stare at this beautiful woman before me.

Mine. All mine.

"Yes," she nods. "I'm all yours. And you're all mine."

I hadn't realized I'd say it out loud. She reaches for me, and we tear at my clothes, needing to remove any barriers between us. I'm panting, ready to devour her, to take her into me and never let her go.

Our mouths collide again, and I maneuver us back towards the bed without breaking contact. I pull back to growl, "Get on the bed."

She rushes to obey, desperate for it. I'm struck by how beautiful she looks: curls dripping wet, eyes wide, skin flushed, nipples pert. She sits with her pussy on full display for me.

I give a breathless laugh. "So needy. You want it so badly. I can smell your arousal from here."

She shakes her head, still panting. "That's not true."

I prowl forward, my eyes devouring her. "Shut up and lay back."

"No." She sets her jaw.

Oh, she *really* wants to play.

I whip forward, grabbing her hips and pulling her to me. She falls back onto the mattress with a startled squeak. I waste no time crawling over her until I'm straddling her head, my cunt hovering over her mouth.

"Lick," I demand. She's shooting daggers at me, but there's pleasure in her eyes, too. I squeeze my thighs together. "Careful, little one. I could squish your head between these tree trunks of mine."

She scoffs, her breath teasing me. My stomach tightens, desire spiraling through me as I watch her feeble attempt at dominance. Now it just depends on who is going to give in first.

A devilish look crosses her face, giving away her intention to fight back some more. Now, that won't do. I lash out, grip a fistful of hair at her scalp, and drive my hand into the bed, making her tilt her head backwards. She lets out a gasp, her eyes glazing over.

"Behave," I snarl at her before pressing myself against her lips.

Her mouth closes around my clit gently, hesitantly. She desperately wants to please me, so worried about not doing well that it throws her off.

I close my eyes for a moment and let out a moan, encouraging her. That seems to help—she lets out a mewl against me and moves her tongue over my clit more confidently.

Pleasure sparks along my skin, making me pant as Danielle starts exploring me. Her tongue massages my clit a few more times before she dips lower, licking at my opening. She looks up at me with a nervous look, trying to figure out what I like, what will get me off.

It's erotic, seeing her so concerned with my pleasure. She might want to play this reluctant character, but what she really wants is to be good for me.

I swivel my hips, softly riding her face. Arousal spreads through me as she moves back up, her warm, wet tongue circling my clit. "That's it, Danielle. You're so good at this."

She whimpers against me, her eyes closing as she drinks from me. Her hands grip my thighs, keeping me in place as she takes her fill. She feasts from me, her mouth making my arousal climb higher and higher. We both lose ourselves in the pleasure, reduced to two animals.

"That's it," I say tightly, release gathering where she's working me as I grind against her tongue. Her soft moans fill my head, making it impossible to focus on anything else.

One final slow, languid lick and I implode. My orgasm shatters me, breaking me down until I'm no longer a person, but just mindless, endless sensations. I chase the high, not ready for it to end, riding Danielle's face like there's no tomorrow. She holds me to her mouth, as needy for it as I am.

As I put the pieces of myself back together, I peer down and take her in—her eyes, softened with pride at getting me off; her dark hair framing her angelic face like a dark halo. A halo for a goddess of pure, carnal pleasure.

I climb off her and stand on wobbly legs, stepping away from the bed to rifle through my bag that I left by the door to find what I want.

A sinister grin graces my lips once my fingers graze it.

"Wh-what are you doing?" she asks in a hushed tone.

I turn to face her, a large dildo and harness in my hands. "You didn't think we were done, did you?"

Chapter 40
Danielle

My mouth dries as I take in the massive toy Blair is holding. "That won't fit," I sputter.

She chuckles darkly. "I'll make it fit. I'll make you bleed if I have to." She walks to the end of the bed before pulling the harness and the dildo into place. "Come here. Legs up."

I don't even consider disobeying. I scramble to the edge of the bed, laying on my back. My hands wind around the back of my thighs, spreading myself wide.

Blair growls and tilts her head. "Perfect."

My body is on fire. I got wound up from pleasuring Blair, and now I might combust. She positions the toy at my entrance, and I buck my hips, wanting it, needing it now—

The tip stretches me wide, and my eyes roll into the back of my head. "Oh God," I moan. I stare up at her and feel fear mix with desire.

A slap lands on my pussy, startling me back down to earth. "There is no god," Blair snarls from above. "There is only you and me, and that is all we need."

She slams into me, her hips flush with mine, the cock spearing me, splitting me in two. I cry out, my body teetering between pain and pleasure. She doesn't let me acclimate before she starts moving in me, setting a punishing pace. My body goes limp as pleasure overtakes me, overwhelms me.

Blair grabs my legs and pushes them into my chest, somehow making the toy move deeper in me than before. I'm not going to survive this; the pleasure will destroy me, will set me ablaze until I'm just ashes floating in the wind.

"It's too much," I plead.

"You'll take what I fucking give you." Her hand slaps my clit again, and my arousal spikes. "What do you say to me for fucking you stupid?"

My toes curl at her question. "Thank you, Daddy."

"That's right." Another slap. "You want to come all over Daddy's cock, don't you?" *Slap, slap.*

Fucking Christ. "Yes," I pant, my orgasm growing at an alarming pace.

"Beg me to let you," she commands.

My babbled pleas fill the air as release continues to grow. If I don't come soon, I might die. Sounds I've never made spill from my lips as Blair abuses my pussy, letting pain and pleasure dance in me. She doesn't offer any reprieve, doesn't give me permission.

"Please," I cry, tears pooling in my eyes. "Please, I need to, I need it, please—"

"I give you exactly what you need," she grunts, hips slamming into me again and again.

"Yes, yes—" I'll say anything, agree to whatever she wants—

"You're mine. Mine forever."

"I'm yours," I whimper. "Please, please let me come."

Another slap lands, making me scream. "Come on me, Danielle. Soak me."

My back arches, muscles straining, cries leaking from me. I might die from this—I don't know how I'll survive—

The final slap hits my clit just right. My orgasm wipes my mind of all rational thought, leaving only earth-shattering arousal in its wake. I'm not going to survive, but I don't care—

Blair slams to the hilt and I feel myself flutter around her. "There you go," she encourages. "Feels good, doesn't it?"

I can't even answer; no words enter my brain. I'm still riding the high and I'm never coming back down.

She leans forward, pressing my legs harder into my chest, nearly folding me in half. "This is the most beautiful thing I've ever seen," she murmurs before leaning down to brand me with a kiss.

Chapter 41

Blair

Danielle is gathered in my arms, her still-damp hair soaking my shoulder. "I'm going to have a bird's nest in the back of my hair," she groans.

I hum. "I'll brush it for you."

"Then I'll look like a poodle."

"I see no problem with that," I say, which gets me a playful snort.

My phone buzzes on the nightstand. I detangle myself and check the screen.

A message from Cherry:

Wasn't us. Assumed it was you.

"What is it?" Danielle asks.

I put my phone down and lean against the headboard. "Have you seen the news about those murders in town? Well, no bodies have been found, so technically, they're just missing. The victims are all men around the same age."

"Yeah, I have." Her tone has a nervous edge. "What about them?"

I shrug. "I thought I knew who was committing them, but they just told me they weren't."

She's silent for a moment. "You know actual killers?"

"Of course I do."

"Oh," she whispers.

"Does that upset you?" I ask.

"No, it's just...you've talked about killing Jeremy, and part of me didn't think you were serious."

Ah. "You're now realizing I'm dangerous. That I meant what I said."

"I knew you were dangerous, I just..." She chews on her bottom lip for a beat. "How many killers do you know?"

"A few." *Not counting myself.*

"Do you ever..." She sits up, her eyes glued to her lap. "You once said people tell you morally questionable things and you don't judge them. Have you ever judged someone for killing someone else?"

I blink, unsure of what she's getting at. "It depends, I guess," I say. "Depends on the circumstances, their motivations."

"But if someone was killing bad people, that would be okay?" she pushes.

"It isn't about if it's okay or not—realistically, I don't think I care enough." My brows raise at her line of questioning. "What's this about?"

She takes a deep breath and lifts her eyes to mine. "You *do* know who has been murdering those men. It's me."

My mind short-circuits. "What did you just say?"

Danielle's dark eyes drill into mine as she straightens, her shoulders rolling back. "I killed the men that have been disappearing."

I struggle to comprehend what she's telling me.

She continues, "I started because...because I wanted to know what it would feel like, to end the life of someone so horrible, so vile. These were bad men who did terrible things to people. I wanted to enact my own justice. I also wanted to practice, so that when I finally face Jeremy...I'll be ready. I knew I couldn't face him yet—it would make me feel frozen, seeing him.

"It would remind me of all the times he hurt me, belittled me, controlled me. But if I killed someone else, someone just as evil, just not to me...well, I thought it would help prepare me."

That is the sexiest thing I've ever heard. "And did it? Prepare you?"

She shrugs. "I don't know. I still haven't gone home to do it, so I guess not."

"How did you find these men?"

"There's a group online that exposes shitty men in your area. I would swipe on dating apps until I found the right ones."

"But…how? I've been watching you…" I wrack my brain for any instance of her disappearing into the night.

She squirms a bit. "Once I had the security system, I got nervous. I stopped for a while—until I figured out how to alter the camera feed."

"You didn't want it documented where you were going," I guess, something that feels an awful lot like pride sitting in my chest.

"I looped the footage quite a few times."

I want to kick myself for only noticing it once. "Are these your first kills?" I ask, hungry for the details.

She takes a breath before nodding. "I never had the courage to do it before, but I've thought about it. Day-dreamed about it, even. But I was too afraid of get-ting caught to follow through. Besides, no one has ever wronged me enough to consider murder. Until Jeremy."

My heart is beating wildly in my chest and my palms are slick. I feel like I could run a marathon.

"But these men," she continues, "while they haven't wronged me, they've wronged others. They've harmed women *like me*. They deserved to die."

That's incredibly sexy. I have a little killer on my hands.

Our future is limitless.

"They did," I agree. "And you were the one to enact justice. How did it feel?"

"It felt..." She seems to struggle with finding the right words. "It felt wonderful. Powerful. Right." Her eyes show hesitation. "Is that bad?"

"No," I answer truthfully. I know the feeling very well. "That's why you don't want me killing Jeremy—because you want to be the one to do it." She nods. "If I'd have known that, I would have happily given it up," I tell her.

"So, you don't...think less of me?"

"Never." I reach forward and grip her hands. "You said these were bad men, right?"

"Yes," she replies.

"Then you're making the world a better place." I squeeze her palms. "My first kill was my father." The words shock me. I had planned to tell Danielle at some point, but not until I thought she was ready.

I guess my radar is off.

I continue, "He wasn't abusive, or mean, or even a bad person. He hadn't laid a hand on any of us. I did it simply because he left me with my mother, and I didn't care for her. I found his decision to leave to be the wrong one."

"Why didn't you kill your mother instead?" she asks.

I huff a laugh. "I nearly did. But Ariana needed a mother. I didn't want to deprive her of that, even if she wasn't the best parent in the world."

"How did you kill him?" Her eyes alight with curiosity.

"I shot him. I didn't need it to be a long, drawn-out murder. It was just to see how it felt to kill." Danielle waits for me to keep going. "And I didn't feel anything." I shrug. "I felt like I made the right decision, but I wasn't excited or happy or regretful."

Her thumb rubs the back of my hand. "I get what you mean. The men I kill don't bring me anything other than a feeling like the world is less horrible."

"It is," I tell her. "Society is full of bad people."

She nods in agreement.

"We're meant for each other," I breathe. I think this woman has made me feel shock for the first time in my life. "We are perfectly matched."

"You know, I think you're right." Her dimple appears as she smiles, and I feel my world tilt on its axis.

Making breakfast for Danielle may become a ritual. I love feeling her gaze on me as I move about the kitchen, how enthusiastic she is about the plate I serve to her.

Her dark eyes light up as I place a stack of pancakes in front of her. "I've always been shit at making these," she murmurs before diving in, ignoring the steam radiating off them.

I sit down next to her, more interested in observing her than anything. After a few mouthfuls, she peeks over at me sheepishly before swallowing.

"They're good," she mumbles.

Shrugging off the praise, I ask, "What should we do with our day?"

Danielle hums, looking past me for a moment before her face turns mischievous. "I'd like you to take me on a motorcycle ride."

My eyebrow quirks. "Have you ridden before?"

She shakes her head, her curls bouncing around her. "Nope, but I want to."

"It'll be a cold ride," I muse aloud, mostly to myself.

"Oh." Her face falls a bit. "That's okay. Maybe another time."

I snort. "Just layer up."

Danielle's face lights up and she gives me an excited peck on the cheek before rushing out of her chair towards the stairs. "Aye aye, captain," she shouts, taking the steps two at a time.

Shaking my head, a smile crawls across my mouth as I stand and put our dishes in her sink. Swim Shady peeks his head out of his hiding place, as if sensing me. I can't resist this little fish.

"It's becoming obvious that you're getting extra food, you know," I whisper conspiratorially as I sprinkle in a few pebbles.

I hear Danielle racing down the stairs a few minutes later, looking like a giant snowball. My eyes drag down her body, noting multiple layers of clothing swallowing her frame, and tilt my head.

"You'll need the use of your arms," I inform her.

Her eyebrows furrow. "For what?"

"To wrap around me."

She blinks and looks down at herself before she reaches her arms around herself in a hug, but doesn't quite make it.

"I could lose a layer or two," she says before throwing off her light knit sweater, exposing a gray sweatshirt underneath. "Better?"

I nod. "Let's go."

We get our coats over us and shove our boots on before stepping into the chilly morning. Danielle and I step off her porch and I grab her hand, guiding us down the street to where my bike is parked.

As we near, Danielle asks a bit nervously, "Do you have helmets for us?"

"Mine is locked to the bike, which you'll be wearing."

"I don't want you to go without one," she argues.

I peek at her from the corner of my eye. "I'll be fine. We won't go far."

She chews on her bottom lip, not seeming convinced as we reach the motorcycle. I drop her hand and unhook the helmet, turning to her with it outstretched.

"Come here." She obeys quickly, which makes my blood heat. I place the helmet over her head, securing it in place before pressing a kiss to the top. "Step back for a moment."

I turn and throw one leg over the bike, settling into place before bringing it to life. It thrums underneath me, the engine singing as I rev it. I look at Danielle and jerk my head. "Climb on, baby."

If she's nervous, I can't tell through the visor. She strides forward and climbs up, straddling the bike and throwing her arms around my middle. One of my hands squeezes hers before I place them both on the handles.

Twisting my head, I say loudly, "Lean with me."

And we're off. I hear a little squeak and feel Danielle press her front into my back, clinging to me for dear life.

I take us down her street, wind biting at my face. I throw myself into the turn, taking us right, letting our speed accelerate quickly.

Riding without a helmet is extraordinary. I turn my head slightly and shout, "Enjoying yourself?"

A peel of laughter greets me before she yells, "This is amazing!"

We're speeding down side streets, which only makes Danielle laugh harder. A satisfied grin spreads across my face, enjoying this more than ever before because of her.

Her hands glide up my chest, feeling me up as we race through the neighborhood.

I'm pondering how we could successfully scissor while operating the motorcycle for the rest of the ride.

"I'll be back," I tell Danielle a few hours later. "I just need more clothes."

"Why can't I go?" she pouts.

"Because it's too far and you'll get cold," I argue. "I won't be gone long."

She sighs but doesn't push it. As much as she loved the adrenaline rush of the ride, the wind was harsh today.

"Don't take too long," she murmurs, eyes dipping to my mouth.

Grinning, I capture her lips with my own. We grab at each other, breathing life into the kiss. Too soon, I pull back and promise, "I won't leave you for long," before stepping out into the cold winter night.

We're perfectly aligned. It's poetic, really—two killers falling in love.

Is this what I've been missing out on? I feel weightless and there's a goofy grin on my face that won't go away. I already miss her and need to be near her, even though I just saw her.

This all-consuming feeling makes my existence finally feel worth something. Danielle was right—I *am* able to feel, to some extent. Now that I do, I never want to feel anything but this.

I hear Danielle's steps behind me. She must miss me already, too.

Turning, I say, "Looks like we both—"

I don't get the rest of my words out before something slams into my head, knocking me off my feet. Pain explodes behind my eyes, making me see white as I land on the ground.

I try to lift my head, but a second blow comes, and I'm dead to the world.

Chapter 42
Danielle

Happiness has me floating as I move around the house, waiting for Blair to come back. She only left a few minutes ago, but I want her back here immediately. It's as if a thread connects us, and it's taut as we get further apart.

But then I hear the front door open.

I let out a giggle as I move into the foyer. "That was fast."

"Not fast enough."

My blood runs cold. That voice doesn't belong to Blair.

The figure enters the front door and slams it shut behind.

Jeremy stands in the doorway, dead-eyed, a bloody baseball bat in his hand.

I freeze, my mind going blank with panic.

A smirk slithers across his face. "Not happy to see me, Dani?"

My mouth opens but no words come out. I feel like I've been transported into my nightmares, but I don't need to pinch myself to know it's real.

He steps closer, and I immediately back up. Thoughts slam into me, trying to get my body to work, to focus.

How did he find me? Where's Blair?

"Your cunty friends shouldn't post everything online," he sneers. "They basically posted your address for the world to see."

My heart is racing so fast, it's going to give out. My vision is starting to tunnel. Phantom pains crawl across my body—reminders of how and where he's hurt me.

He scratches his temple with the top of the bat. "You know, I would've let you go. You weren't worth anything anymore. But then you *ran*." He spits the word at me. "You thought you could just leave me and start over somewhere else?"

His laugh makes my stomach twist.

"What do you want?" I gasp out.

"I just wanna talk." He shrugs, pretending like we're just old friends catching up. "Just like old times. What do you say, Dani?"

I'm going to throw up. "S-sure." I keep myself facing him as I back us into the living room.

"Aw, sweetheart, there's no need to be scared." His dead eyes crawl over me, making my blood feel like oil in my veins. "Sit."

He rounds the couch as I lower myself into the chair across from him, my eyes ping-ponging between him and the bat he's gripping.

He lets out a sigh as he sits. "Like I said, I was going to let you go. You weren't even a good fuck anymore. But you just had to make it worse for yourself." He shakes his head, as if in pity.

Where's Blair? My mind starts shouting. *Where is she?*

Jeremy keeps talking. "I can't believe you're going to make me do this. You are the reason I'm doing this, you know. You brought this on yourself."

Where is Blair? The voice in my head is taking over, I can barely hear his rant over it.

"Did you see a woman leaving my house?" I interrupt, unable to wait any longer.

Jeremy's face contorts with anger, but I need to know. "No," he grits out, his jaw clenching. "Can't even pay attention to me for one fucking minute."

His empty hand balls into a fist. He's clearly holding back from hitting me—until he's gotten his speech out.

"You're sure?" I push, trying to rally my nerves. "She's tall, got dark hair. She had her motorcycle parked outside. You didn't see anyone?"

"God fucking dammit, Danielle!" He stands abruptly and flips my coffee table over, sending candles and books flying. I recoil, pushing myself into my seat to avoid the attack. "I don't give a shit about your little friend, and neither should you. You should be begging for your sad, pathetic life." He points the bat at me to emphasize his words. "You should be on your knees, crying, pleading with me—maybe even sucking my—"

Jeremy flies forward, falling awkwardly on top of the wreckage of my coffee table. He lands with a crash, and the bat skitters across the room.

And behind him stands Blair, blood dripping down the side of her head. Danger and rage ooze from her, darkening the entire house, like an angel of death.

Without hesitating, I rush for his weapon, but a hand wraps around my ankle, bringing me to the ground. I fall on top of books and glass, pain spreading through my abdomen. I pivot and kick Jeremy in the face. His nose breaks under my foot. He releases me with a shout, and I crawl to the only thing that would give me an upper hand.

My fingers close around the bat as I hear Blair and Jeremy enter into a battle behind me. I shift onto my back, just in time for me to see Jeremy's hands wrap around Blair's neck.

My wrath breaks free of me as I pick myself up, weapon clenched in my fist, and throw every ounce of anger and desperation into my swing.

Chapter 43

Blair

If I wasn't injured, I would have stood a better chance—but this dude is massive.

He charges me, his hands around my neck as he slams me into the ground, looming over me. His breath smells of whiskey as he snarls, "I'll kill you too, bitch. I'll bury you two together, won't that be nice?"

He squeezes the air from me, and I'm already getting lightheaded. My vision clouds around the edges. If I pass out, that'll be it for me. I try to push him off, but my limbs aren't working.

A deafening crack fills my ears and the pressure on my neck immediately stops. I suck in air greedily and turn myself on my side, trying to put as much distance between us as possible.

Jeremy is on the floor beside me, a loud moan leaking from his mouth as he grips his head.

Danielle stands above him, bat in her hand, a murderous expression on her face.

I try to speak, to tell her to shut him up once and for all, but only pained gasps come out. My throat burns, making it feel like I'm breathing fire.

Danielle brings the weapon down upon his head a second time.

Silencing him—for now.

She stares down at him for a moment, seeming to process what just happened, before her dark eyes snap up to mine. A sob slips past her lips as she discards the bat next to her unconscious ex and kneels beside me. Her hands delicately brush against my temple, my throat.

"Blair," she cries. "You're hurt. We need to take you to the hospital."

I shake my head as I sit up. *No hospital.*

Tears fall down her cheeks as she sees the damage he's done to me. Her lips replace her fingers, kissing my injuries gently, reverently.

"I'm sorry," she whispers against my skin. "I'm so sorry, I'm sorry."

My mind is moving a bit slow, but I manage to direct my mouth to say, "Not your fault." The words are gravelly.

Danielle pulls back. "It is. He's here because of me."

I hate seeing her like this; I don't want to hear this from her. Wrapping my arms around her, I gather her to my chest. We sit together among the wreckage, her crying softly into the side of my neck, her hands gripping the front of my coat.

"Shh," I whisper, rocking us back and forth. "It's all right. We're all right."

I hold her until her cries die down and she pulls back, eyes red and face splotchy. "Do you think anyone heard us? What if the police show up?"

"I don't know," I answer, my brain trying to get itself sorted. "We need to remove him."

She turns to look down at his limp body beside us. "He isn't dead. He'll wake up soon."

I nod. "Let's get to work."

Chapter 44

Danielle

Dragging a limp body is no easy task. I grabbed his legs while Blair gripped him under the arms. We took him into my basement, a space I've only been using for storage. It's damp, with concrete walls and flooring, and only one hanging light bulb that sends shadows skittering across the room.

We dropped his body unceremoniously into a lone chair and secured his ankles and wrists. I gathered some plastic tarps I keep stashed down here, surrounding him.

Now, I chew on my nails, anxiety overtaking my senses. I have my abuser with a bashed-in skull in my basement. My former kills have done nothing to prepare me for this moment like I'd hoped they would.

I can't do this.

Blair returns from upstairs with a glass of water in her hand. Her throat must be killing her.

"What do we—"

Before I can get my question out, she strides toward Jeremy and throws the water in his face. He jolts awake, sputtering as the water washes over him.

"Time to wake up, fucker."

Jeremy looks around, eyes wild. "What the fuck?" He tugs on the restraints keeping his arms tied behind him.

"You're tied to a chair," Blair states calmly, walking over to place the cup on the boxes stacked behind me.

"You fucking bitch," he seethes, his eyes trying to melt the skin off my face. "I swear to God, I'm going to fucking kill you."

My body locks up, immediately remembering each time he'd threaten me—threaten to kill me if I left him or if I told anyone what he was doing to me.

I can't do this, I don't even know why we're doing this—

A gentle touch on my forearm brings me back into my body. I turn my head and find Blair scrutinizing me in her classic aloof way, with anger burning under the surface.

Jeremy is still screaming profanities at me, but I no longer hear them. It's like I've been transported into this alternate reality where it's just Blair and me and no one else can ever come here.

She licks her lips and says, "This is what you've been waiting for."

I suck in a breath, letting her words wash over me. Jeremy doesn't have the upper hand here—I do. If we do this right, he never gets to hurt me—hurt anyone—ever again.

Giving her a small nod, I turn my attention back to the man who made my life a living hell, who took so much from me, who continued to take and take and take until I had nothing left. Who ran me out of my own life.

The fear dissipates, leaving only anger—pure, undiluted anger—in its wake. I step further into the room, letting him see what I've unleashed. He seems to hesitate, his chest heaving as he sucks in air, but he's stopped bitching.

I can feel Blair behind me, pacing like a guard dog, ready to attack for her master.

"Do you remember when you punched me so hard, I blacked out?" My voice is low. I don't need to shout for this. "You gave me a black eye."

As quick as a viper, my fist shoots forward, connecting with his face. His head whips back as my knuckles press into his eye. He howls in pain, but I barely even hear him over the blood pounding in my ears.

Power floods my veins. "Remember when you broke my nose?" I ask before I move again, crushing the already-broken cartilage. I'm breathing heavily, the sting of the strikes fueling me, urging me forward.

Blair steps into view, the baseball bat in hand.

I give her a feral grin as I step away from him. He's crying now, pleading. "Dani, please, I need a doctor."

I ignore his words. "Remember when you broke my arm?" Blair strides behind him, looking at me over his head, looking for confirmation. "It was my right arm."

She nods and undoes the ties to his right arm. Before he can register the freedom, Blair holds his arm straight out, gripping at the wrist, and brings the bat down onto his forearm. A beautiful crack fills the air, followed by his screams.

Blair releases him, which causes another shriek of pain as his arm dangles at his side, useless.

Yes, I think. *This is right. This is what he deserves.*

The world will be a better place without him in it.

Blair lets out a sadistic chuckle, two fingers touching his face gently, gathering the blood already spilt.

She raises her eyes to me, my angel of death and destruction, as she lifts her fingers and drags them down her cheeks, creating tears of blood. She's the most beautiful creature I've ever seen.

Smiles light up our faces simultaneously. *Let's begin.*

It takes three hours to serve my justice. By the end, he's barely holding on. His eyes are swollen shut, blood runs down his broken nose, his arm broken, as are both of his ankles.

Blair and I took turns beating him with the bat, aiming to break at least four ribs. He passed out from the pain twice, but we refused to give him any respite, forcing him awake to feel every moment of agony.

His skin is a sickly pallor and he's having trouble re-acting to the pain anymore. His blood coats the ground beneath our feet.

"He's fading," Blair tells me, but I already know.

I step towards him and grip his hair, tilting his head back.

His eyes droop and a pained moan comes from his bloody mouth.

"You nearly killed me," I tell him. "You took everything from me, and it nearly ruined me." I lean my face closer to his. "But I got away. I get to live my life, and now, I get to take yours."

I hold out my free hand, and Blair provides me with my knife from upstairs—the knife I've used to end lives just like the man's before me. The blade glints in the dim light.

"I will be the last thing you see before you die."

Slowly, so tortuously slowly, I slice his neck wide open. His eyes show his panic, and I drink it down. Gargled noises are all that can escape as he chokes on his own blood.

My body sings as the light leaves his eyes.

Chapter 45

Blair

The mask is off now.

Danielle stands before me in all her bloodthirsty glory, reveling in the life she's ended.

I nearly fall to my knees for her.

She releases Jeremy's head, letting it hang, his dead eyes staring up at the ceiling, before turning to me. I suck in a breath at how stunning she is after a kill. It makes me jealous I wasn't there when she killed the others. I want to be the only person who sees this side of her.

Still gripping the knife, her eyes slide down my body, hunger radiating from them. "It's done," she breathes.

I nod. "We should dispose of him."

She steps towards me, desire etched into her face. "We should," she agrees.

Our bodies collide with urgency, a fire already burning between us as we grab at one another. My mouth descends to her neck, and I bite, eliciting a moan from her. She grips my waist to pull me closer, her fingers dipping under my shirt. We're both broken and bleeding, and I'm fairly certain I have a concussion, but this is all we want now.

My mouth moves up to capture her mouth, and we're a tangle of teeth and tongues, desperate to swallow each other whole, to make ourselves one. She paws at my shirt with one hand, her blood-soaked fingers cupping my breast. I arch into her, needing more, needing it all—

She pulls back slightly to demand, "Get on the stairs," in a husky voice that makes my knees weak.

I obey, backing up until my heels hit the bottom stair behind me. Danielle forcefully, but cautiously, pushes me down so that I'm sitting, and I lean my elbows back.

"I want to fuck you with this." She holds up the knife that she used to end that loser's life.

Arousal sparks in me as I take in the long handle and I nod. An evil grin spreads across Danielle's face at my consent. She drops to her knees and unbuttons my jeans, which I assist with their removal by wiggling out of. My bare ass sits on the step, and I spread my legs wide, inviting her in. "Do your worst."

Danielle places the blade guard on before flipping the knife around. With a seductive groan, she slides the knife handle into her mouth. She eases it in and out, getting it wet for what we're about to do. She holds my gaze as she removes it from her mouth with a pop and brings it to my entrance. I'm already clenching down in anticipation, nearly dripping for it.

Gently, she presses it into me, and I gasp. It's cold and feels strange inside me. She pushes it in, further and further, and holds it still—letting me acclimate to the foreign sensations. Pleasure spirals out of control. I need her to fuck me, harder, faster.

I circle my hips and give her an encouraging nod. Danielle pulls the handle out and slams it into me. My head falls back, the fullness almost overwhelming.

"Fuck," I cry out at the ceiling.

Danielle's chuckle dances over my skin. I'm already feeling untethered, like I'm free-falling.

Until I look back at Danielle, and that thread connecting us goes taut. She pumps the handle in and out, her eyes wide and hungry, as she devours me. I'm reaching the pinnacle too fast; I want it to slow down, to be in this perpetual purgatory of pleasure forever.

"You love this, don't you?" She watches with rapt attention, her eyes darting from my face to between my legs.

A whine snakes from my throat. "Yes," I moan, the pleasure growing out of control.

She gives me an evil smile before leaning forward and swiping her tongue over my clit. Stars dance in my vision as I become overwhelmed with arousal.

"Fuck, that's good," I groan.

Danielle places her mouth against me and moans, the vibrations nearly making me weep. The sound of her lapping at me greedily is one of the dirtiest things I've ever heard.

The handle thrusting into me and Danielle's sinful tongue throw me over the edge. I cry out as my orgasm takes hold and doesn't let me go. Danielle keeps fucking me as I ride her face, never wanting this to stop. I leave my body, floating somewhere up above, lost to the sensations.

When I finally come back down, Danielle gives me one final kiss on my clit and eases the handle from me.

That is now my favorite knife.

Chapter 46
Danielle

I stare down at Jeremy's lifeless body and feel...nothing. All he became was a problem. A problem that hurt me, took from me, made my true self hide in the furthest recesses of my mind. He kept me caged for so long. I wonder if I would have blossomed sooner if he hadn't tried to ruin everything.

Now that the initial glory has passed, I see nothing but a body I have to move.

Blair wastes no time, even though I'm desperate for her to see a doctor. She dismisses my concern, telling me she knows someone who will take care of everything for us.

"What do we do now?" I ask. "Burn his fingerprints off so he can't be identified?"

She shakes her head. "Burning his prints is a waste of time. We'll simply remove his hands and feet, and extract all his teeth. Then we'll sever his limbs and his head so that he can be disposed of in different locations."

Ew. I wrinkle my nose. "I don't love the idea of chopping him into pieces."

Blair shrugs. "And I don't love the idea of going to prison. What did you do with the bodies of your other murders?"

"I would wrap them in a tarp, tie cement blocks to them, and dump them in the different bodies of water in the area."

Blair groans and rubs her temples.

"What is it? Is it your head?" I rush to her.

She waves me off. "No, it's not that. It's just that we'll have to fish those out eventually."

Oh. Well, that sucks.

"A problem for another day." She gives me a smile.

"Hold on. You said you know someone who would take care of this for us. Why can't they just come here and do everything?"

"Because coming to them with a smaller problem is a lot better than coming to them with a big one. Providing them with a body already dismembered is a thoughtful thing to do."

I shrug. "Okay, then. Let's get to it."

Blair stashed an alarming number of blades in *my* car that cut through his body well enough, but it definitely isn't easy—some parts of him required all of our strength to cut through.

She claims she left them with me for this very reason. I would be annoyed, but they're coming in handy.

"Last one," she informs me as she extracts a molar from his mouth with pliers. The tooth makes a plunking sound as it drops into the bowl holding the others.

Jeremy is officially dismembered; his limbs, hands, feet, and torso are wrapped in cellophane, ready to be delivered to who-knows-where. I take the bowl of teeth and dump them into a small, plastic sandwich bag, shaking them a bit to hear them click together, as Blair wraps his head for transport.

"We'll put them in the trunk of your car," she tells me as she grabs his head, "and get it detailed after."

I nod and reach for one of his arms. "He's a lot lighter in this form," I quip as we make our way up the stairs.

Blair snorts.

We load him up silently before I reverse the car out of the garage. Blair grips the safety bar above her window and throws me a startled look.

"Why are you driving like a bat out of hell?"

I furrow my brows. "I'm not. This is how I normally drive."

Blair curses under her breath before telling me to get onto the highway, heading west.

"Where, exactly, are we going?" I ask once I merge onto the nearly empty streets.

She leans her head against the window as she answers, "Her name is Cherry—well, that's what she goes by, anyway."

"And what will this Cherry do for us?"

"She'll get rid of him—his body, but also his life. Make it look like he's fucked off to Lithuania or Australia or somewhere."

"She does all of this herself? How do you know you can trust her?"

"Cherry doesn't actually do any of this herself; she makes calls to people, and those people get it done."

I sneak a glance at Blair and see her eyes getting distant. "Is she, like, in the mafia?"

"Yes."

My blood pressure spikes. "Wait, seriously? You're involved with the mafia?"

"Don't be ridiculous, Danielle. I'm not *involved* with them—not anymore. I just happen to be friends with a woman who is very influential in those circles."

"Jesus fucking Christ," I sputter.

"It's fine," she soothes, but her words come out a bit slurred. I look over and see her eyes closing.

"Hey, hey," I lean over and snap my fingers in front of her face. "Don't pass out on me."

She rights herself and says, "Cherry is a badass. I think you'll like her."

"I want to scream at you for this, but I'll wait until I know you're safe." A twinge of guilt sits in my stomach—we could've held off on fucking to get Blair's injuries checked out.

I look down at myself momentarily, knowing I'll need medical attention too. "Will Cherry get us fixed up?"

"Uhmm-hmmm."

"Blair," I warn, gripping her hand. "Stay with me, okay?"

She interlocks her fingers with mine. "I'll always stay with you."

Chapter 47
Danielle

Blair managed to give directions, and forty-five minutes later, we're pulling up to a massive home with an iron gate.

I roll down the window as I hear, "Name?" coming from a speaker to my left.

"Uh, Blair Erickson?"

The speaker makes a clicking noise, and the gates groan open. I drive slowly up to the property, marveling at the trees and hedges lit for Christmas.

"Woah," I breathe.

The mansion before us sits on top of a hill, with a winding driveway and a small pond in the valley. It looks like a massive doll's house, with numerous windows and a massive wind-around porch. A cylinder pillar juts from one side, and a chimney stands proudly on the other.

As we approach the mansion, a small older woman steps outside, who eyes us like a hawk. She looks to be in her mid-sixties, with chunky streaks of gray in her auburn hair, and a hook nose.

I stop the car and get out. "Hi there, uh, Mrs. Cherry, I'm Danielle—"

"What's wrong with her?" She jerks her chin to Blair.

"I think it's a concussion."

Cherry sighs. "Fine, bring her in."

I rush to Blair's door and open it, my arms reaching to assist her, when she vomits all over the pavement. "It's all right," I tell her even as my anxiety morphs into panic. "Let's get you inside."

Blair mumbles something incoherent as I sling her arm over my shoulders and guide her inside, with Cherry leading us. We're greeted by a giant foyer, with a grand staircase to our left and what seems to be a living room to our right.

"Take her to the kitchen. I don't want her puking on my carpet," Cherry says as she heads up the stairs.

"I don't know where it is," I mutter, dragging Blair towards the back of the house.

I decide to take a guess and walk us straight back. Luckily, we reach the enormous kitchen, where I help her into a seat at the large dining room table.

"Hey," I say gently to her as I kneel in front of her, stroking her hair back from her face. "We're at Cherry's now, and she's gonna get you taken care of, okay?"

She blinks at me.

"At least you're alive," I breathe. A moment later, Cherry walks into the room, flanked by two tall, striking men who look identical, with auburn hair and hook noses. Cherry's genetics didn't play any games here.

One of the men steps forward, pushing his thick-rimmed glasses into place, as he gestures to Blair. "May I?"

Part of me wants to say no. Blair didn't mention anything about Cherry having two very tall, very burly sons. I don't love the idea of them touching her.

"Calm down," Cherry says as she goes to sit across the table. "Christopher's the best doctor in the state."

His cheeks go a bit pink at her praise. "I'm a trained physician. You said she might have a concussion."

I nod. "And maybe some damage to her throat, too. From being choked."

Christopher nods. "I'll need to take a look at her to assess any injuries." His eyes dip to my blood-stained shirt. "I take it you will need medical attention, as well."

"Her first."

He walks towards the kitchen sink, washing his hands deliberately, while I sit across from Cherry, who lights a cigarette.

"So," she starts after taking a drag, "what's the story?"

"Ma," Christopher says as he approaches Blair, who doesn't even react as he places his fingertips against her temples. "No cigarettes around my patients."

"It's my house, Christopher," she gripes, but stubs it out in the ashtray sitting on the table.

"Blair and I need your help," I tell her.

"Well, that's obvious." Her hazel eyes burrow into mine. "She's always getting into trouble."

"We killed someone."

I wait for the shock, or for any type of reaction, but no one in the room even bats an eye. "And?" Cherry prods.

"He's dismembered in the back of my car."

"You want me to take care of it."

"Blair said you're the one for the job."

She huffs. "This girl has been dropping problems into my lap since she was eight. I thought she'd turned a corner when she stopped doing work for me a couple years ago." She cocks an eyebrow. "Maybe you're a bad influence."

I huff out a laugh. Oh, the irony. "Yeah, maybe."

"If I take care of this problem, what do I get in return?"

"What do you want?"

Cherry leans back in her chair, still scrutinizing me. "I'm sure you can guess."

"You want us to kill someone for you?"

She shrugs. "Depends on what I might need that day."

"So, we're indebted to you forever?" I scoff.

She ignores me. "Do you know how I know Blair? I found a tiny girl, dragging my neighbor's dead body through the yard. She took that man's blood and smeared it across her face like some animal. Ultimately, I wasn't surprised by what she had done. I can smell a killer from a mile away." Her sharp eyes scrutinize me. "What I am surprised by, though, is that she brought me another."

"I think we should wait until Blair's recovered before striking any deals," I counter.

Blair blinks at me, but doesn't offer any thoughts, as she clearly isn't present for this conversation.

"You'll stay here until then." Cherry's tone makes it clear there's no room for argument.

"I'd say she has a concussion and injuries from strangulation," Christopher interrupts, "but nothing major. She'll need to rest for a few days. If she has any pain, any over-the-counter medication will do." He turns to me. "Now, let's get you cleaned up."

Chapter 48
Blair

Cherry saved my ass—or rather, her son did.

Danielle and I spent two days at Cherry's, staying in an enormous guest room with an en suite bathroom. Cherry's chef prepared meals for us, delivered to our door so we could focus on rest. The bed alone could fit five people.

I've never stayed at Cherry's before, but I wasn't surprised when I woke up in this bed.

It's obvious Danielle is uneasy being here. She told me what happened after she dragged me inside, as my memory is fuzzy from that point forward. I've got a concussion, but nothing life-threatening. Danielle had some cuts but is healing nicely.

She also shared how Cherry basically said we owe her, which isn't a shock to me. Every time Cherry has gotten me out of sticky situations, I've always had to pay her back. I've smuggled drugs a few times, but the rush of that got old quickly, so we moved onto killing people.

Looks like I'll be doing that again.

Danielle sits beside me in bed, chewing on her fingernail. I gently ease it from her mouth and lace our fingers together. "Why are you worried?"

"Because this is a mobster's house," she whispers urgently.

"You can speak at a normal volume."

"She wants us to kill people for her."

"So? We *just* killed someone, and you've apparently been doing vigilante shit behind my back."

"What if she has *us* killed?"

I lift our intertwined hands and kiss her skin softly. "She won't. Believe me, I've come to her with way worse and she's been fine about it." She doesn't seem convinced, so I give her a devilish grin. "Think of it as an adventure. We get to kill together. No more having to do it on your own. I saw how horny killing made you—I can still feel the handle inside me." I shiver.

She narrows her eyes, but she can't stop the smile that breaks across her face. "Who, exactly, is Cherry?" she asks, trying to ignore my attempt to rile her up. "I thought only men were in charge."

"Oh, they are. Cherry's husband, Anthony, is high up there, but she's the brain working behind the scenes."

"Will we have to answer to him?"

"In a way, but I've always dealt with Cherry—or rather, she's always dealt with me," I explain. "She was a smart choice for a wife. The story goes that he saw a young, hot Cherry out with her cousins, and Anthony knew he had to have her. He tried courting her, but she knew he was bad news, so she never returned the sentiment. Well, he got tired of it, so he kidnapped her."

Danielle's eyes go wide and her mouth pops open. "He *what?*"

"Mmhmm. Snatched her right off the street on her way home. He held her hostage for a few days. Now, he claims he treated her like a queen; showered her with diamonds, expensive clothes, and even a dog." I snort. "But she was having none of that shit. So, she ran home. Problem was, everyone knew what bad business Anthony was into. When she went home, her parents wouldn't let her in. They basically disowned her, right then and there. Anthony scooped her up and they've been together ever since."

Danielle shakes her head in disbelief. "That's a classic case of Stockholm Syndrome."

I shrug. "I stalked you and you fell in love with me," I point out.

"That's different."

"Sure, it is."

Danielle sighs. "I never wanted to learn how people end up in situations like this."

I'm struggling to follow her line of logic. "What's the difference between your previous murders and these future ones? It's still killing, just with more protection."

"Because I was killing for *me*," she emphasizes. "I was choosing my victims. I got to decide. Everything was my decision." Her dark eyes look...sad.

I release our hands and sit up, throwing a leg over so that I'm straddling her. My hands cup her face as I lean forward to share her breath. "You may not get to pick them, but you'll still be killing bad people. People who don't deserve to live." My eyes dip to her nose, her lips. My thumb caresses where her dimple currently lays dormant. "While I love what a vicious killer you are, I want you to be safe. As I've told you before, I have no interest in prison."

Her lips quirk. "You're saying murder comes with a perk package."

"Yes," I breathe. "Benefits that can help keep you out of harm's way. I think this could be a good thing. You may lose your choice in victims, but it will still scratch the itch."

Her eyes search mine for a few moments, our breath intermingling as I watch her watch me. "But I get to do it with you?"

The words, the vulnerability in them, nearly knock the air from my lungs. "Always. I will never let you out of my sight."

She relaxes at my words. "Okay," she finally says.

Cherry is in her movie room with her rat-dog, Pepper. Pepper is a scraggly terrier that should've died years ago. I'm convinced Cherry made a deal with the devil to make him live forever.

He has no teeth, so his tongue lolls out the side of his mouth, and his eyes are milky white due to cataracts. His annoying yip starts as we enter the room, and Cherry shushes him by petting his head. The screen plays some old sitcom that my mind is having trouble recalling the name of.

I'll blame it on the concussion.

A stream of smoke rises in the air as Cherry takes a drag of her cigarette. "Glad to see you're awake."

"Tell Christopher that I appreciate it," I say as I sit in one of the leather recliners. Danielle goes to sit next to me, but I pull her onto my lap. She perches, unsure of how she should behave.

"Nice of you to cut up the body for me," Cherry comments.

I shrug. "It was my pleasure."

Cherry rolls her eyes. "Now that I've scratched your back, it's time to scratch mine."

"I'll kill whoever you want me to, Cherry, as long as Danielle and I are together. No solo missions. No other mafia shit. Just good ole-fashioned murder."

"Making demands now, are we?" She taps her cigarette against the ash tray propped up on the chair's arm.

"You know that's what I'm best at. The other stuff gets dull."

Cherry jerks her chin to Danielle. "And you?"

Her dark eyes dart to me before saying, "I'm good with that."

"Good. Your car and house have been scrubbed, and we made it look like that man bought a one-way ticket to Aruba." She takes a puff. "Go back to your normal lives, but be ready whenever I call."

I nod. "Understood." Danielle and I get up, heading to the door, when I remember something. "Oh, this isn't that big of a deal, but I might need your help with a few other bodies..."

Chapter 49
Danielle

Going back to my normal life feels strange. I killed the man who tormented me for so long, and now I'm tied to a very powerful—and very dangerous—family.

Having Blair by my side makes it all seem less terrifying.

She doesn't let me out of her sight. I've tried to go back to work, but she refuses, grabbing my waist whenever I try to leave.

"I'm going to get fired," I say, but she brushes off my concerns.

"Your boss's boss's boss is telling you to stay in bed, so that's what you'll do."

We spend the week in my house, barely getting out of bed. Cherry's team did a full sweep of the basement and living room, removing any evidence of Jeremy and the struggle, but it meant losing a few pieces of furniture.

Which means Blair and I are off to IKEA.

I fiddle with the radio as Blair drives. "You're sure you don't want me to drive?"

She gives me a look. "I've seen how you drive, Danielle."

"I drove us to Cherry's with no issue," I point out, feeling a bit offended.

"The only reason I let you drive then was because I would've gotten us killed. Even then, I think our driving skills were about equal."

I huff and cross my arms. "Whatever." Blair chuckles in reply.

We sit in comfortable silence for a few moments before I ask, "When do you think Cherry will call us?"

"Eager to get to it?"

"Not really. I mean, what you said was true; I can still kill bad people. I just hate the uncertainty of it all. When I found my victims, the circumstances were all up to me. But now? Now I have to answer to the damn mafia."

Blair's hand glides across my thigh and squeezes gently. "It will be an adjustment, but you might come to enjoy it."

I purse my lips.

She continues, "You won't have to dispose of anyone; there are clean-up crews for that. You no longer have to find bad people, as they'll be provided to you. And Cherry will be good to us if we're good to her. We behave, and she'll eventually say our debt is paid. Then we can see how we feel."

"We?" I look over at Blair's profile.

Her eyebrows flick up. "Cherry or no Cherry, you aren't doing any of this alone anymore."

The words make warmth spread through my body. "It's like when couples start doing the same hobbies together."

Her lips quirk. "Exactly."

I settle into my seat, feeling a bit better about the situation we've found ourselves in. I can let go of a tiny bit of control if it means doing things safely and efficiently.

My phone vibrates in my pocket, bringing me from my thoughts. I pull it out and groan when I see MOM on the screen.

"Are you going to answer?" Blair questions.

I hesitate, the pros and cons dashing through my head too quickly for me to really process. Without thinking, I answer the call and press the phone to my ear. "Hello."

"Oh, hi, honey," my mom gushes. "I'm so glad you picked up. I was getting worried you were ignoring my calls."

"I was," I calmly tell her.

She sputters, "Now why on Earth—"

"I don't want you calling me anymore." My mask has slipped off. Maybe it never went back on. "This will be the last time we speak to one another."

"Oh, Danielle, don't be so dramatic."

"I'm not. Our relationship ended when you took Jeremy's side over mine. He used to hit me, Mom. I never told you because, deep down, I knew you wouldn't believe me. And if your own mother won't believe you, then what's the point?"

Silence. "Danielle, I'm not sure what this is about, but I'm sure it's all a misunderstanding."

I huff a laugh. "Exactly."

"Your father would be rolling in his grave—"

"Good," I shoot back. "He was a piece of shit, anyway. He doesn't deserve eternal rest or whatever you believe in. And neither do you. Don't call me again."

Before she can say anything else, I hang up and block her number. Closing my phone, I put it back in my pocket and let out a breath.

"I'm glad that's over."

I can sense Blair scrutinizing me. "Are you?"

I wait for any sadness, any anger or regret to come up, but they don't. "All I feel is relief," I answer, because it's true. I look at Blair and give her a reassuring smile. "Honestly, that was long overdue."

"It was," she agrees before squeezing my thigh.

I picked out a sensible coffee table and a few random IKEA things, like shark-shaped ice trays and a Tärnaby table lamp. Afterwards, Blair starts the drive to her place to pick up a few things.

As we cruise down the highway, I ask, "Are you going to be moving in with me?"

"Of course," she answers without hesitation.

I blink. "Oh. You answered that really quick."

"We could move into a new house, if you'd prefer."

I snort. "No, I like my house."

"Good. Besides, your home is already safe for your dietary needs."

"Oh, I've lived with people who eat gluten before, it's totally fine," I argue.

She frowns a tiny bit. "That's ridiculous. I'll be moving into your home and adopting your diet."

"Blair, really, you don't have to."

"Your health and safety are my primary concerns," she replies. "It's the least I could do for you."

My heart squeezes. To have someone do that for me feels monumental. "Thank you," I whisper, not even sure what else to say.

By the look she gives me, words aren't even necessary. We just feel each other, and that's all it takes.

She takes an exit towards downtown, and we pull into a parking lot a few minutes later. The building before us is a large condo complex, each with a balcony and floor-length windows.

I let out a low whistle as Blair parks. "Fancy."

She rolls her eyes.

Climbing out, we walk hand-in-hand to the building. Blair pulls out a key card and taps it to a sensor in front of the entrance, pushing the door open after a loud beep sounds. Our feet pitter-patter across the glossy tile down a bright hallway, an elevator at the end.

"Do your neighbors know about you?" I ask as we step into the open elevator.

She shakes her head. "It's none of their business." The doors slide closed.

"Considering you probably have a shrine of me, I'm assuming you don't have people over much," I joke, watching the numbers continue to climb as we ascend.

"I don't have a shrine," she argues. I can feel her eyes burrowing into the side of my head. "But if I did, I'd happily worship at it."

I scoff, even as my cheeks heat. Before I can think of a witty retort, the door opens, and Blair is leading me by the hand down the hall.

"I'm not attached to this place. I'd much rather be somewhere with you."

"I'd like that," I murmur, squeezing her hand in mine.

We stop outside one of the unit doors, Blair placing her key card against its sensor and pushing the door open.

An industrial-style, open concept space greets me, with exposed pipes lining the ceiling. The kitchen is off to the side, all appliances and countertops the same shade of gray, with the living room directly in front of us. The place looks staged for a tour, with furniture that looks barely touched and artwork that isn't meant to evoke any reactions.

"I bought it staged," Blair says as she lets go of my hand and strides towards a door on our left.

"I didn't say anything."

"I could feel your judgment."

I let out a chuckle and wander into the sterile living room. "It's a bit disappointing, is all."

"How?" she shouts from what I assume is the bedroom.

I step in front of the floor-to-ceiling window that over-looks the parking lot. "I don't know, I just expected, like, weapons and dead bodies strung up in here." I reply loud-ly. "I'm also shocked there's no shrine—even though you did say you didn't have one."

A few beats of silence. Then, "Come in here."

The tone makes my toes curl. I pivot and nearly run into the other room.

Her bedroom is the same as the rest of the apartment: monochromatic. A large bed sits against the far wall with a dresser against the other.

The one interesting part, though, is the desk that sits to my left.

Multiple monitors cluster on top of the desk, all show-ing different areas of my house. I step closer, studying each one, noting feedback for each room, my garage, and different angles from the outside.

She really was watching my every move.

"It was intoxicating, watching you." Her voice slithers into my ear, her body pressing into my back. Instinctively, I melt into her. "Getting to see you, simply existing, was erotic. I can't tell you how many times I've pleasured my-self while watching the cameras."

Fuck. My eyes flutter closed as her arms wrap around my waist, keeping me against her. "It's so wrong," I whimper playfully, knowing full well we both find it hot.

Her nose skims the shell of my ear as she murmurs, "You're just a helpless, little girl, aren't you?"

Oh yeah, I like this roleplay. "I am," I breathe. "You don't watch me get undressed, do you?"

"I do. Every single night," she growls, her hands moving up to cup my breasts.

A tiny moan escapes past my lips. "And do you watch me...touch myself?"

Her fingers circle my nipples through my shirt, making them pebble. I lean my head back, the flames of arousal kindling inside of me.

"It's my favorite thing to watch."

Without warning, she grabs me by the hips and spins me before stepping back. I'm about to object when I see the desire swirling in her eyes.

"Take off your clothes, Danielle."

It isn't until I reach for my shirt's hem that I realize my fingers are trembling—whether from arousal or fear, I'm not sure.

When it comes to Blair, it's usually a mixture of both.

I rip my clothes off, desperate to get some relief from the tension building between us. I need her to touch me, to lick me, to do anything she wants to me.

Her eyes track down my naked body greedily before demanding, "Get on your knees."

I sink to the floor, nerves mixing with giddiness in my stomach.

"Good," she rumbles, before striding out of the room.

I hear her rummaging around and the distinct sound of running water, making me furrow my brows. I consider getting up to peek at what she's doing, but I don't want to accidentally snap the rubber band that's wrapped around this moment and break the spell, so I settle against my heels.

Blair struts in a few moments later, a bowl in one of her hands. A devious smirk is on her face as she bends and places the bowl in front of me, water sloshing over the side.

"Are you thirsty, baby?"

I blink, my mind too hazy with lust to understand. "Am I thirsty?" I repeat.

Blair is a dark, powerful force standing over me. "That's right." She nods to the bowl. "If you're thirsty, you should take a drink."

My eyes dart from the bowl and back up at her, the realization dawning on me. "Oh," I pant, the fire of arousal bursting in my body. I lick my lips and slowly get on all fours, hinging forward until my mouth is at the bowl. With my eyes still holding Blair's, I stick my tongue out and lap at the water.

"Very good," she praises, cocking her head as she watches me. "You like being my pet, don't you?"

I nearly choke on the water. "Yes," I whimper, the arousal becoming too hot, too unruly—

Blair glides to the dresser, temporarily disappearing from view, as she seems to search for something. I hear her shuffling things around before she pops back up, a squeeze bottle in one hand and what looks to be an anal plug in the other. I start sitting up as she comes back around, but she rushes toward me, her foot planting in the middle of my back.

"Don't you dare."

Her boot doesn't leave my skin until I settle back down, my face hovering over the bowl. "What are you—you're not going to—"

"You already know I'm going to do whatever I want to you," she scolds as she moves to kneel behind me. "Keep drinking, baby."

Hesitantly, I lap at the water, suddenly *very* aware that my ass is out on display as something cool starts to drip against the hole. I shiver, both from the sensation and the anticipation.

"Have you done this before?" she asks as something caresses me back there.

My body instinctively locks up. "No—I mean, yeah, like twice, but—" Blair pushes the plug into me, and my eyes roll into the back of my head. It feels strange, like I'm being stretched apart.

She eases it in and out slowly, letting me adjust. "It's small," she comments, "so it won't hurt. I don't want to break my pet just yet."

My pussy clenches with each shallow thrust, and before I'm even aware of it, I'm rocking back and forth, seeking more.

"That's it," she encourages, the plug going deeper each time until it's completely seated in me. Blair flicks the end of the toy, making me whimper, as she cackles. "Looks like I have an anal slut on my hands."

Without warning, I feel Blair's tongue glide across my clit, and I let out a long moan. The feeling of fullness, paired with her tongue expertly circling my clit, is sending me into overdrive. I fight to keep my head from falling forward into the water—though there are way worse ways to go out than this.

Blair laps at me just as I lapped at the water, her lips moving down to suck gently on me.

"I know you need to come," she teases. I rock my hips back and forth as I don't even think I have the ability to speak right now. "I knew this would make you feral."

She's not wrong. I try to hold back, but Blair flicks the plug again, and I detonate. My orgasm burns through me rapidly, making me gyrate against her face with abandon. Blair doesn't let up, her tongue still working against my clit as my release crests, then breaks.

I'm a panting, slobbering mess once I settle; my legs feel like jelly. I look over my shoulder and see Blair has sat back on her heels, her mouth wet from tasting me.

The sight makes me clench around the plug, still deep in my ass.

She must see what she's doing to me, because she gives me an evil smile before diving back in.

Chapter 50
Danielle

I grip Blair's hand as we walk up her sister's walkway to the front door. "What if they don't like me?" I wonder aloud for the thousandth time.

Blair rolls her eyes. "They will. Besides, it doesn't matter if they like you."

I snort. "I still would prefer to be accepted by them."

"The only one that matters is my sister, but even then, it wouldn't change how I feel about you."

We step up to the front door and she gives me a quick kiss on the cheek before she knocks.

A very pregnant woman answers the door with two children peeking behind her legs. She pushes the screen door open with a huge smile.

"I'm so glad you two could make it." Ariana's eyes glitter as she takes me in. "It's nice to finally meet someone that Blair is willing to bring home!"

Blair snorts as her niece exclaims, "Mom, *move*! I need to show Auntie Blair my new dolls!"

Ariana steps back, letting us pass through the threshold before Blair's niece and nephew start buzzing around our feet, peppering us with information about their toys that I can't quite keep up with.

Blair's sister interrupts, "Guys, go play with daddy, okay? I think he's downstairs in his playroom."

His playroom? I fight the urge to shoot Blair a look. The two energizer bunnies rush down the hall as I say, "Thank you for inviting me. You have a lovely home."

I feel a gentle pinch on my ass, as if to say *suck-up*. But Ariana sighs and rubs her swollen belly absentmindedly.

"That's so nice of you to say. We try to keep it clean-ish."

"Are you going to keep us standing here?" Blair quirks.

"Oh, sorry! Yes, please, take off your shoes and get comfortable."

Once our shoes and winter coats are off, Ariana leads us into the living room. The couch and armchair are worn, with a couple stickers stuck to the side. She eases herself slowly into the armchair, leaving Blair and I to sit next to one another on the couch.

"When are you due?" I ask politely.

"Don't get her started," Blair murmurs.

"I'm due any day now," Ariana beams. "I almost had to be induced, but my blood pressure went back to normal, so now I just have to wait."

"I'm sure you and your husband are very excited," I offer.

"Oh, we–"

The sound of elephants running up the stairs interrupts us, just before Emma and Jack burst into the room, their father on their heels.

"Dave," Ariana chides. "I wanted you to watch the kids while I chat with the ladies."

"The kids are hungry," he grunts, making my hackles rise.

Blair told me a bit about Ariana's husband, but it's different to see it for myself. Yeah, I don't care for him.

"Danielle, would you mind helping me in the kitchen?" Ariana asks. "I've made up some snack plates for everyone."

I give her a warm smile and say, "Of course." I squeeze Blair's thigh before standing up and following her sister into the other room. I hear Emma talk excitedly as we enter the kitchen. A few bowls have been made up, full of chips and popcorn.

"Blair told me that you can't have gluten. Is everything here okay for you to eat?" she asks nervously. "They were all labeled gluten free, but I wasn't sure."

"Everything looks great, thanks so much."

"So," Ariana starts, turning to face me before leaning her hip against the counter. "How did you two meet? My sister was tight-lipped about any details–minus your dietary restriction."

"Oh," I say before clearing my throat. "We met on Halloween, and then realized we worked together." *Sort of.*

"What a coincidence." She licks her lips nervously. "I've never met any of Blair's partners, so I hope you don't think I'm being too forward, but..." I raise my eyebrows. "It's just..." she sighs. "I was beginning to think she'd never find anyone, that she's too...different for a relationship."

"Different how?" I ask, even though I'm very aware of Blair's...uniqueness.

She shakes her head. "She's always been different. She never really had friends growing up, but the ones who would befriend her always ended up leaving the friendship in tears. I watched her manipulate others around her—other kids, teachers, neighbors, whoever she could get her claws into."

I bristle at her words. "I'm not sure what you're getting at." My tone is sickly sweet.

Her voice lowers as she continues, "It's just...it wasn't until my husband asked me if she'd ever hurt animals that I started to wonder if maybe she's..." She bites her lip.

"Maybe she's what?" I press.

"That maybe she's sick. Not right." She swallows, showing her discomfort.

Rage burns through me. Blair's brother-in-law is making Ariana question her? I don't like that one bit. I force a smile to my face. "Blair may be a bit unconventional, but I'm positive she's never hurt anyone." Has she? Of course, but I'm not about to say that. "She's nothing but loving to my fish," I say light-heartedly.

Ariana's eyes show her relief. She laughs a bit. "I'm happy to hear it. And I'm happy she has you. I get good vibes from you."

I need to have a talk with Blair about her sister's radar for people. It's clearly on the fritz. Forcing another smile, I say, "Let's bring these snacks out. Don't want anyone to get hangry out there."

Ariana and I step back and each grab a bowl, making our way back into the living room. Blair's niece is informing everyone about the drama between her dolls as I place a bowl down on the coffee table. Sitting beside Blair, I put my hand on her knee and press a kiss to her temple. She turns her head to look at me, blinking in surprise. I shake my head slightly to say, *we'll talk about it later.*

I meant what I said—Blair is unconventional. She scared me at first, but that was before I understood her. She doesn't want to hurt me and would die protecting me.

To think her own blood doesn't understand her makes me want to whisk her away, to hide her from their judgments.

She might want to protect me, but I will happily step up if she's in harm's way.

Blair's phone buzzes in her pocket. She takes it out and peeks at the screen before excusing herself into the other room.

I have a feeling I know who's on the other side of that call.

I slide onto the floor next to Emma, who allows me to play with her dolls. "This one is Sarah," she informs me. "She really wants a haircut, but her mom said no."

"You can't give your dolls haircuts, baby," Ariana sighs.

Blair steps back into the room a few minutes later, her face carefully blank.

"Everything all right?" her sister asks.

Blair nods, her eyes trained on me. "Just work. Looks like that deliverable is needed by next week."

My heart starts racing. "Do we have all the information we need?"

"The client will send everything over tonight."

Ariana's husband snorts. "Who knew marketing was so high stakes?"

Epilogue
Blair

A Year Later

I hear Danielle shout, "Done!" from upstairs, which means it's time to move.

Cherry called this morning with our newest target, a rival who stepped into their territory. He was found trafficking children through the city.

I can't wait to make him suffer.

Danielle and I had only planned to pay off our debts to Cherry and move on, but we came to really enjoy working together and not having to worry about the logistics; we just go in, murder, and walk out.

So, Danielle pulls any information she can on them before we attack. But I have more pressing things to do now.

I stand down the hall from her bedroom, my mask firmly in place. She's already talking by the time she enters the hall. "I'm excited to—" Her eyes land on me, and she halts.

Time to play.

"No," she gasps, backing up into the bedroom. "No, stay away from me."

I chuckle under my mask. I love when she plays my helpless victim.

She spins and darts into the bedroom, and my primal side breaks free as I haul ass after her. I burst into the bedroom and catch her around the waist as she tries to hide in the bathroom.

"Where do you think you're going?" I laugh in her ear as she fights against me.

"Get off me!" she screams, giving me a good fight.

I wrestle her out of her clothes, my hands roughly grabbing her as she tries to get away. I throw her onto the bed, and she pivots to face me, her eyes alight with desire, even as she pants and crawls backwards.

I grab one of her ankles and pull the rope from my back pocket, quickly securing her to the bedpost. The desire has won out in this little scenario—she's stopped squirming as I tie her other ankle and her wrists to the bed, keeping her spread wide.

"What are you going to do to me?" she whimpers.

A laugh bubbles out of my throat. "I'm going to make you mine."

I dip into the closet and pull out our sex toy box, grabbing her favorite vibrator and the gag with a dildo on the other end.

"You know the rules," I remind her as I saunter back over. "You're not to come until I say so." I fit the gag into her mouth, securing it around the back of her head. "Tap the headboard once if you're going to come, and twice if you need to stop. Understand?"

She nods, the cock wiggling with the movement. I quickly tie the vibrator to her leg, making sure it's in the perfect spot to tease her.

"I love edging you," I murmur as I turn the toy on. Her hips buck, and I press my palm against her lower stomach. "You always cry, and you're so pretty when you cry."

Moans leak from her gagged mouth, and her eyes are wild as she watches me strip down, removing the mask, and straddle her face. The tip of the cock brushes against me and I shiver.

"Let's see how many times I get to come before you do."

I sit down on the toy, its girth stretching me nearly to the point of pain. I keep my eyes on Danielle's, which are hazy with lust, as I bring it to the hilt. "Oh, baby," I groan, rising up slowly before slamming back down. "Having you underneath me makes me wild."

She mewls in response, her body writhing. I start fucking myself in earnest, pleasure taking over me as I bounce on the toy.

Danielle shuts her eyes, and I snap, "Keep your fucking eyes open. I want you to see what you do to me."

She quickly obeys, her dark eyes bursting open before she taps once on the headboard.

"Oh," I snicker, pivoting to turn her toy off. "That's why you closed them, hmm? You couldn't hold out any longer. At least you listened."

I rotate my hips, keeping the toy deep inside me, letting it hit the spot that makes arousal spark through my blood. "Once you calm down, I'll turn it back on."

I have to turn Danielle's toy off three times before I consider showing her some mercy. Tears stream from her eyes, muffled pleas on her lips. She's bucking her hips, desperate to come.

I move faster and faster, bouncing myself against Danielle's face. "So pretty," I pant, my eyes tracking the newest tear that slides down her temple. "So perfect."

Release builds in me, making me feral. "Do you want to come, my love?" She whines, her entire body shivering. I let out a breathy laugh as I reach the edge of my orgasm. "Come for me, baby."

She goes over the cliff of pleasure, and I fall with her. Her muffled screams are like music to my ears, making my orgasm grip me and turn me inside out. My head falls back, and I cry out at the ceiling. We writhe together, primal animals lost to our instincts. Nothing is better than this.

Except for killing together.

Once we both settle, I pull myself off the cock, and release Danielle. She stays limp on the bed, drunk off pleasure, as I ease the gag from her mouth. I lay down next to her and pull her into me, my arms securely around her.

"I love you," I murmur into her dark curls.

She burrows her face into the crook of my neck and breathes, "And I love you."

Epilogue
Danielle

Something wraps around my wrists, tugging them together. My eyebrows pull together as I try to separate them.

"Stay fucking still," a voice growls at me.

It's enough to shake me awake. I had been cleaning with Blair for the afternoon, and told myself I would nap for only a few minutes.

Apparently, those few minutes have cost me.

My eyes fly open to total darkness. Something is covering them. "What the fuck?"

Blair doesn't bother answering me—she binds my wrists together, and before I can protest, I'm being hefted into the air. My stomach hits something as I'm bent in half, the sound of Blair's boots pounding against the hardwood telling me that she's hoisted me over her shoulder.

"What are you doing?" I screech, bouncing as she carries me somewhere.

"Be quiet, or I'll gag you."

Even though this is a disorienting thing to wake up to, desire flits in my stomach.

Until I hear a door open and I'm deposited roughly onto the ground. "See you soon." I can hear the evil grin in her voice before the sound of a door closes and I realize she's locked me away.

I lift my tied hands to my face and rip off the eye mask to find I'm in the trunk of my car.

"Blair!" I shout and start banging on the ceiling. It does me no good—I can feel the car rumble to life and we're off.

I'm fuming by the time the car finally shuts off, all but forgetting this is some kind of sex-capade, and I'm shouting bloody murder when the trunk door opens. I rear my foot back and kick blindly, my foot connecting with something soft. I hear Blair grunt, and I'm brought down from my anger enough to realize what I've just done.

Blair stands above me, her mouth bloody, eyes murderous.

"Oh shit," I gasp, scrambling to get out of the trunk. "I'm so sorry, I didn't mean to—"

"You're going to pay for that." Blair spits blood on the ground before grabbing my arms and roughly pulling me from the car.

I don't have a chance to inspect the damage before she shoves the eye mask back in place.

Fear dances along my skin as I'm led stumbling away from the car. The gravel under my bare feet causes pinches of pain, which will pale in comparison to what Blair will do to me.

"Where are we going?" I ask, considering laying down on the ground in an act of defiance.

She doesn't bother answering, but her grip tightens on me. After an eternity, I hear a door open, and I'm thrust into a room before the door shuts behind us. Blair continues to drag me until she pushes me down. My front hits something soft and springy—a mattress.

"Did you take me out into the middle of the woods?"

"The mountains," she corrects from behind me.

"Oh. I love the mountains," I say, trying to act like this is totally normal.

"I knew I should've gagged you," she murmurs dangerously. "Get up on the bed."

I obey, squirming until I'm lying flat on my back, staring up at the darkness of the eye mask.

"Arms above your head."

I do it, arousal mingling with the fear as my wrists are secured to what I'm assuming is the bedpost.

"Blair, I'm really sorry for kicking you—"

"Save it," she snarls before I feel her fingers curl into the waistband of my sweats. "You want to act like an animal, then I'll fuck you like one."

My pants are ripped from me, exposing me to the cool air. I shiver, both from the cold and her promise. I strain to hear movement, any indication of what she's doing, but she's silent. It makes me wonder if she's left the room. "Are you still there?"

No response.

"Blair?" My voice wavers. "Okay, I get it, you're trying to scare me. It's working." A little, nervous chuckle passes my lips.

I don't hear anything for several moments except for my breathing, which is getting faster and faster each second. If she tied me up and left me like this as some kind of prank, I'll be livid.

"Seriously, Blair—"

Before I can finish, something is shoved into my mouth. I sputter, trying to dislodge it, but it's no use. It doesn't have a taste, but its texture feels like cotton on my tongue.

"My underwear is the perfect gag for you."

Blair's voice finally reaches my ears just as the bed dips by my feet. She grips one of my ankles and she pushes my leg up, forcing it to bend at the knee, before something presses against my clit. It doesn't vibrate, but it's warm and wet. I clench around nothing as it starts to move against me.

"Even after all this time, you're still so misbehaved. My training seems to not be working."

"I take offense to that," I try to reply, but it comes out garbled. What's pressed against me picks up speed, making me feel desperate to know what it is. I gyrate my hips, wanting more friction.

"Would you like to see what I'm doing to you?" she asks, and I whimper, nodding my head profusely. Then the eye mask is gone, my eyes squinting against the flood of light.

To see Blair grinding her pussy against me.

Lust floods my system, rendering me useless except to be a limp toy for her pleasure. I watch with rapt attention as we glide against one another, making me hot with arousal.

"This cabin is for us," she growls. I'm not even sure what she's talking about—I'm too lost in where we're joined to think of anything else. "No one will hear you scream up here."

My eyes roll back in my head as desire overtakes me.

She keeps going. "This is where I'll breed you. I'll find the best specimen. I'll tie you to this bed and shove it right into your greedy hole, and I'll watch you get swollen with our baby."

Fuck. I focus back on Blair just in time to see her eyes glaze over, her free hand splaying across my stomach possessively.

"Mine," she snarls.

Release blooms in me, but I can't warn her. I try to hold it back, to know I can't come without permission, but I don't think I can stop it.

All I can do is mewl as she rubs herself against my clit.

Blair's head falls back, and her stormy eyes shut as she lets out a long, deep moan, her orgasm overtaking her.

It throws me over the edge—release slams into me, whisking me away, pulling me from my own body as we writhe together. The pleasure rides me forever, not letting up.

Blair keeps scissoring me, her eyes devious. "We aren't stopping. I deserve to come a hundred times after the little stunt you pulled."

My moans sound pathetic as I let her use me. We're both wet, the sounds of us sliding together filling my head.

"I'm sorry, I'm sorry," I mumble, the words incoherent, but I can't stop.

Blair growls, "I'm going to fuck you until I get my fill, so be quiet and take it. You'll come so many times, you'll be begging for it to stop."

My eyes squeeze shut as release starts to gather at my spine. She's going to force orgasms out of me.

I'm never going to survive this.

My body is wrung out like a used sponge.

Blair didn't let up, fucking the life out of me to the point of pain. I found myself dreading each building orgasm.

She's found an effective punishment.

I'm stretched out on the bed like a starfish, taking in the mountains out of the floor-to-ceiling windows as I come down from the heavens. Blair struts over to me, placing a steaming mug on the nightstand before crawling into bed.

She gathers me in her arms, propping us against the headboard. Her fingers gently massage my scalp, making me nearly purr.

I turn my head and peer up at her to find her gray eyes studying me. Without a word, we meet each other in the middle, our lips caressing in a soft, intimate kiss.

I never knew I could be as happy as I am now, in the arms of someone who understood me better than I did, who helped awaken who I really am, and who will always be by my side.

We pull back slightly, our eyes holding one another contently, the silent words flowing between us.

I reach up to caress her mouth when something shiny catches my attention.

There's a ring on my finger.

I blink at it, not comprehending where it came from. Blair's chuckle tickles my ear. "I put it on you while fucking you. I think you were too distracted to notice."

I can't even conjure a memory of this happening. I marvel at the dainty diamond on my ring finger. "You knew I was going to marry you," she continues. "It was just a matter of when."

Snorting, I put my hand on her chest, my eyes softly closing as I settle back against her.

Blair was right—it's just her and me, and that is all we need.

Acknowledgements

This book has helped me more in the past six months than I thought possible. I started writing it pre-November 2024 election, and it helped carry me to today.

I want to thank my beta readers, Gigi Zarbi, Annmarie, Aida, and Katherine, for seeing the vision of these two unhinged women.

Thank you to R.N. Barbosa, who literally swooped in to save the day. Thank you for taking such good care of Blair and Danielle (and me).

Thank you to Annmarie at CBC Editing for proofreading, and for not judging me for never knowing the difference between lay and lie.

Thank you to Erika Karr, my PA, for literally everything. I wouldn't know how to navigate half of this shit without you.

Thank you to the authors before me who have written unhinged stalker MCs. I eat that shit up and always want more.

And a thank you to you, my readers. Having so many of you (im)patiently wait for this book has been surreal. I hope you'll stick around for what's coming next.

9 798991 028639